DREAM
WRECKS

D I C K   H E I M B O L D

To Ulla, Christa, and Mike

and

Memories of Ron

ACKNOWLEDGEMENTS

Heartfelt thanks to good and patient friends—Ben Curtis, Ted Kalmon, George Scribner, Bruce Trentham, Diane Carter, Erin Heimbold, Eric Heimbold, Katerina Geringas, and Francesca Murphy—who helped launch me on this journey.

Chapter 1

DREAM WRECKS

Mitch slumped into a chair and wailed, "Another goddamn Dream Wreck—I need a better…"—he dropped his head into his hands, stifled a sob—"a better way to live." After a few moments, he lifted his head and spoke into his dark studio space. "Jesus Christ, Mitch, get your ass in gear."

Quiet for a moment, Mitch stared into the memory of a savage Afghanistan firefight that was still virulent from his nightmare an hour ago. Gathering what remained from his inner strength, he stood up and faced the paint spatters on the canvas.

In his wild abstract painting, the troops in their foxholes were greenish-black daubs of paint. They were straining to see in the dark. Looking in the enemy's direction. He took a bristle brush and smeared on paint—silhouetted enemies looming closer. He dunked a round brush in liquid oil paint and slung white spatters across the canvas—tracers arcing out—seeking enemy flesh. Then he slung red spatters of relentless incoming rounds seeking American flesh. He saw shapes charging out of the night. He felt mortar blasts he knew would kill if they landed near him.

He dealt hot steel to furtive forms cutting through the barbed wire—right from the tube. He squirted words on the canvas in whatever color he grabbed: "INCOMING, SHIT, POUR IT ON." He spackled thick, white layers near the top, when flares lit up the night. Rampant emotions flowed onto the wild color forms. His battle raged through two hours of high-intensity painting, and then the combat flashbacks receded. Mitch whispered, "We beat them back. They're retreating."

He stood back to look at his work. After silently scrutinizing every part of the painting Mitch stepped forward to spread final color shapes on the canvas with a palette knife. The painting became more real than the receding nightmare memory. Fighting the urge to overwork his raw strokes, Mitch stopped painting and lifted the wet canvas off the easel. He propped it against the wall in the morning light and studied it intently. Finally he said to himself, *Yeah, it's finished.*

———

Mitch Alexander's morning routine started three months ago. It was at an art therapy workshop at Mount San Gorgonio Veteran Rehabilitation Center in Palm Desert. There he learned that instinctive, physical painting was an antidote for the ravages of "Dream Wrecks"—his name for the nightmares that ravaged his nights.

He discovered that pouring out a nightmare's horrors and panic into a Dream Wreck painting made him feel better. A Dream Wreck painting delivered relief—until the next night.

The paintings had to be completed before a normal day opened up for him. If he didn't get to that point when something inside said, "You're finished," then the day could still be plagued with depression or anxiety.

He painted fast—an ability well appreciated at the Art Center in Pasadena, his alma mater. At Mount San Gorgonio, he could complete a Dream Wreck painting well before lunch, then go on to a normal day. A normal day amounted to taking care of personal needs, attending meals with fellow patients, handling assigned chores, participating in group therapy, exercising, reading, and associating with others without friction or conflict.

Mitch started painting a Dream Wreck every morning. After racking up a month of normal days, the psychological evaluation staff determined he was good to go. Dream Wreck paintings were his ticket back to the real world.

When he left Mount San Gorgonio, Mitch moved to the Brewery Lofts—a warren of industrial buildings gathered beneath the looming Pabst tower in the industrial area of LA. The Brewery's brick eminence, grown comic in its old age, lent an easygoing quality to life in the lofts.

Mitch had his life under control—sort of—thanks to guidance by Dr. Burt Philorubius, the VA therapist who got him into the Brewery. Burt knew Mitch graduated from the Art Center and wanted him to get into an artist's environment. He wanted to see Mitch's fledgling expressions of creativity, interrupted by war, given a chance to bloom.

Three months later Mitch was still keeping it together mentally. He phoned Burt when emotional storm clouds gathered or visited him when depression's thunder rumbled in the distance. The nightmares persisted at the Brewery, but cranking out a Dream Wreck in the morning fought off the demons for the rest of the day.

His dingy studio was starting to fill up with Dream Wreck canvases. Stacked high, the canvases gobbled up a lot of room. Mitch carved out pathways to his stove, sink, cot, and bathroom; not much space was left for his easel and worktable. *They are serious works,* he thought as he viewed the stacks of paintings. *They could sell if people would just connect with the emotion I put in them.*

Talking to himself as he sponged off at his sink that was filthy from paint, thinner, and neglect, he said, "Man, you gotta sell some Dream Wrecks." He paused. "Or get a bigger studio." He paused again. "Yeah, like I can afford it on disability."

He toweled off, pulled on a denim shirt and jeans, and slipped his feet into flip-flops. He walked to Barbara's café down the alley. It had just opened. Kathy the waitress was straightening tables and chairs. Dressed in a peach-colored nylon uniform with a white apron, she was flitting around on white, thick-soled shoes when Mitch walked in.

"Hi, Mitch, another tough night?" she asked and filled a cup with coffee.

"Medium crappy," said Mitch, sitting at the counter where Kathy put the cup.

"Medium—sounds like you're making progress," said Kathy, as she wiped off a table.

"How'd you like to *buy* a Dream Wreck?" Mitch asked.

"Can I buy it cheap, with nothing down and long-term financing?"

"Sure," said Mitch. "A hundred bucks—or best offer."

"You mean it?" asked Kathy, as she positioned a napkin holder in the center of a table.

"Yep."

"Bless you, Honey." Her oval face lit up. "Can I pick any one I like?"

"Yep," said Mitch. "Any one you like. Pay when you can."

"You walking around again today, Hon?" she asked, looking concerned.

"Na, doin' therapy at the VA. Bus comes any minute."

"How about a bear claw? Get your blood sugar up." She took it out of the pastry case, knowing he'd say yes.

"Can't resist high-end junk food," said Mitch.

After the last bite of bear claw and final slurp of coffee, Mitch stood up, and said, "Bye, Good Looking."

"Bye, Hon. Take care."

He headed for the bus stop in his least-spotted pair of jeans.

Kathy watched him through the window. She liked his walk because he stood up straight and looked like he knew where he was going.

Chapter 2

BREAKTHROUGH

At the VA complex, Dr. Burt Philorubius got a cup of coffee from a vending machine. He was on the way back to his office after his morning trip to the john. Overloaded with cases, he tried to give his best to the never-ending stream of America's sons, shuffling back from the wars. Waiting for him would be Mitch Alexander. He'd been nudging Mitch back to normalcy with antianxiety and antidepressant pills, counseling him in small doses, because of an impossible caseload, and offering him a lot of useless empathy.

Mitch's support system wasn't great. An only child. Mother dead. Estranged from father for years. Relatives in the Midwest not close and mostly still disgusted with his self-destructive behavior after leaving the marines. The doctor was quickly shuffling through the manila folder holding Mitch's file, when his door opened and Mitch came in. After shaking hands, Mitch sat in the chair facing Burt's desk. He looked dejected.

Burt asked, "Still Dream Wrecking?"

"Yeah, painted another Dream Wreck this morning."

Burt said cheerfully, "It got you going."

"True," Mitch said. "Got me out of bed. Got me walkin' around. Got me here."

"Your paintings got you out of Mount San Gorgonio," Burt reminded Mitch.

"Roger that. That's the good news."

"It takes time to take the next step toward living your day in a more productive way."

"How much time?" asked Mitch.

"Hard to say, but you need time for building your confidence."

Mitch shifted in his chair, leaned forward a little, and said, "I want to live more like—normal."

"Dream Wreck paintings are a catharsis," said Burt. "Each one gets negative energy out of your brain. To tell the truth, I think they are damned good."

"What do you like about them, Burt?"

"They are no-bullshit paintings," Burt said.

"What's that mean?" asked Mitch, sounding testy.

"I'm no art critic, but they look like you are putting real…" Burt groped for a word. "Er…*anguish* on the canvas. I'd hang more here, if I had space." Burt glanced around his office, admiring the two Dream Wrecks on the walls.

"Jesus, Burt, glad you like them," said Mitch, getting louder, "but I need more than waking to a freak-out painting every morning then walking around for the rest of the day. I want to make a living!"

"You've come a long way…"

Mitch raised his voice to a shrill, desperate level. "I'm goddamn tired of being the tour guide on the Under LA Walking Tour." Then he faked a happy voice and said, "Lotta sprawl—seen it all." He took a long pause, looked directly at Burt, and said forcefully, "Listen, Burt, I want to think about nookie again. I want to have a girlfriend! I wanna stop being a friggin zombie!"

Burt slapped his desk. He shouted, "That's great! I've been waiting to hear that for months."

Mitch, astonished, leaned back in his chair and said, "You're shittin' me."

"No shit, Mitch. Erotic imaging is a manifestation of that wonderful life force in all of us—the force that takes in love and expresses love. Your condition in recent years has suppressed this force."

"Got that right."

"Just now you told me the force is once again surging. You have the psychic energy for meeting the challenges of everyday life—and for cutting loose your creative forces."

"OK, Burt, don't start hyperventilating."

"Well dang, Mitch, I am wildly excited because I see good things in store for you. This is an important development. Pretty soon the only thing sick about you will be your jokes." With that Burt burst into uncontrolled, loud laughter.

"Burt, you are not instilling confidence," said Mitch frowning.

"Sorry, man. I get such a kick out of my own jokes," he said, suppressing more laughs and wiping his eyes.

After waiting for Burt to simmer down, Mitch asked, "What's next, Burt...for me?"

"Art therapy," said Burt matter-of-factly.

Mitch groaned with exasperation and slapped the arm of his chair. "Burt! Enough with the lame jokes."

"No joke, my man. You're going to Malibu Beach to see a guy named Chad Willoughby..."

"Chad in Malibu. Sweet," said Mitch sardonically.

"He is a top-notch art therapist who is doing great things with talented people—people like you, who are ready to fly again—ready-for-launch people who just need the right catalyst for lift-off."

Mitch, who couldn't suppress a smile, leaned forward, putting his clasped hands and forearms on the edge of the desk, and said, "Beam me up, Burt."

"OK, pal, here's the deal," Burt explained. "Monday morning take the bus out Pacific Coast Highway to Corral Creek Bridge."

"Bus?"

"You'll see a bunch of artists across the highway from the bus stop. That's Chad's group. He'll be expecting you between nine and ten, because I am calling him as soon as we finish. It's a long ride, but you can handle it."

"Thanks...I guess."

Mitch left and headed for the bus stop.

———

Burt called Chad Willoughby and asked him to take Mitch into the Monday group—two days away. Chad agreed—said he could squeeze him in.

Next Burt called Surfer Cobstone, a fifty-year-old, wave-riding fixture along Malibu's twenty-seven miles of shoreline. He jokingly asked Surfer, "You keeping out of jail?"

"Yeah, Burt. Good to hear from you."

"Working?" asked Burt.

"Most of the time. I help Chad with his group. Get a few bucks for that. Do quick sketches on the Malibu pier. Frogs really go for them. In fact I'm at the pier now," said Surfer.

"Frogs?"

Surfer said, "Frog tourists appreciate fine art, *merci beaucoup*. Sell a painting now and then. Stuff like that."

"Where are you living, Surfer?"

"I know what you are pulling at. No, not homeless—got a room at a ranch in Malibu Canyon. In return I feed the horses."

"That's progress, kiddo," said Burt, always looking for the sunny side of the lives of his former patients.

"Why the call, Burt? You want the money I owe you?"

"Nope. Got a favor to ask of you."

"Wuz 'at?" asked Surfer, looking out to sea, wondering what it would be.

"Got a guy coming out to Chad's group."

"What's his name?"

"Mitch Alexander," said Burt. "I want you to keep an eye on him."

"Why's 'at?"

"He's still a little shaky," said Burt.

"Is he using?"

"Not a doper. I just want him to stick with Chad's program."

"What's his problem?" asked Surfer.

"He's got a three-hour bus ride from downtown to Malibu."

"That sucker needs a car," said Surfer.

"You got it," said Burt.

"What's that got to do with me?"

Burt with phone propped between shoulder and ear, closed Mitch's file. "I want you to make Malibu enjoyable for him. I want him to get motivated, buy a car, and stick with it. He's a vet—another vet, like you, who you can do a lot of good for."

"OK, Burt, I'll bring your boy along."

"By the way, Surfer, this guy's got talent."

"For painting?" asked Surfer.

"Yes," said Burt, "Art Center grad. Knows what he is doing."

"OK, I'll check him out and send him back to you if he sucks," said Surfer with a grin on his weather-beaten face.

"Thanks, Surfer. I knew you'd come through."

———

Later back at Barbara's café, Mitch was pecking at Kathy's laptop. He said, "I'm checking bus schedules. Headin' for Malibu."

"Malibu?"

"Yup, Doc Philorubius is putting me into an art therapy group there. Says it will cheer me up—could even get me some sex."

"Hey, Mitch, if I wasn't married to my own artist nut case, I'd clean your pipes and save you the three-hour bus trip."

"Holy shit, you're right. I have to take three buses. Takes two hours thirty seven minutes." He paused and looked up from the laptop. "Have you considered a divorce?" Both broke out laughing.

"Mitch, go for it. You need a change from the Brewery."

"Ya think?"

"Uh huh," said Kathy as she moved off to take care of customers.

"I'll need a hat to keep the sun off me," Mitch said on her return.

"You'll look just like Indiana Jones," said Kathy, exaggeratedly fluttering her eyelashes in approval.

"Long bus ride," said Mitch.

"Time to take off your training wheels and buy a car," said Kathy with an impudent twinkle in her eye.

"Aw, come on, Kathy. Stop flirting with logic. How about a burger and a beer?"

"OK, Mitch. Shall I drag it through the garden?"

"What?" he asked, looking puzzled.

"You want salad?" asked Kathy, writing on her order pad.

"Yes, dressing on the side."

"What kind, Hon?"

"Blue cheese."

"How do you want it cooked?"

"Medium."

"Fries."

"No fries."

"Coffee?"

"Yes."

"Got it."

Kathy turned toward the kitchen window and called out, "Burger, missionary style, garden drag, blue moon in a side-car, eighty-six the fries, and draw one.

Chapter 3

MALIBU

Mitch took the three buses to Malibu. To his surprise the moving view of the city from his window in the buses was a treat—a break from hours of walking that filled most of his days. The moving panorama started with the gray industrial area that includes the Brewery Lofts. Then the bus trip proceeded through the downtown with its budding arts district, convention center, sports arenas, and other new, colorful places. Going west across town, he saw miles of nondescript urban dwellings scrolling by his bus window. He also saw the enclaves of prosperity becoming more numerous as the bus got closer to the sea. Eventually the bus hit the edge of land at Santa Monica, took a right, and headed up Pacific Coast Highway.

The beach scene favored other breeds—joggers, bicyclists, swimmers, surfers, sunbathers, and just plain walkers—than he was used to seeing on a daily basis. Sitting on the ocean side of the bus going up the coast, he took it all in and tripped out on the parade of images—especially the pelicans.

The pelicans cruised along above the breaking waves or along the cliff edges with almost no effort. *But after all,* he thought, *they have been around since the Ice Age, with no change in appearance, and they have this flying thing down pat. Read somewhere they stopped evolving thirty thousand years ago. I guess because they could do everything they wanted to—as well as they wanted to.*

The pelican reverie ended when the big, orange bus stopped at the Corral Creek bus stop. He got off and saw a group of artists at easels across the street. A burly guy, with black horn-rimmed glasses and big straw hat waved to him. Mitch sprinted across Pacific Coast Highway to the ocean side, with an irate motorist blaring his horn while shouting "Knucklehead!" at the near miss.

"I'm Chad." He extended his hand. "You must be Mitch."

"Can't you find a safer place to paint?" asked Mitch, while shaking hands.

Chad chuckled and said, "Man, if you can stay alive, you'll love it here."

"I'm ready for the cure," said Mitch. "What do you want me to paint?"

Chad gestured toward the expanse of the coast and said, "Paint what you see."

Mitch eyed the other artists' works. They all painted the beach scene realistically. He said, "Chad, like, I don't do oceans. I am more of an abstract artist—if you know what I mean."

"Everyone here is at some stage of being pissed off at me for making them paint ocean, beach, and sky. But, keep in mind that Plein Air Expression is the most successful modality in psychotherapy today," said Chad a bit unctuously.

Maybe he is kidding, thought Mitch. He responded, "Aren't you laying it on a little thick, Chad?"

"Yeah, I am," Chad said with a grin, then pointed to an empty easel. "There is an easel set up where *you* are going to lay it on as thick as you want. Burt told me you went to art school before the marines."

"I can only do the ocean?" asked Mitch with a frown.

"You can do ocean, beach, sky—anything you see looking along the coast.

"Also Burt told me you work fast, so I am expecting good things from you. At one o'clock we break for lunch across the highway at Malibu Seafood."

———

Laying into the oils, Mitch went for capturing a breaking wave. Halfway through his painting, he saw a surfer catching a ride. He painted him in his picture. The same surfer paddled near him to beach his board. From his backpack, he pulled out painting gear, set up next to Mitch, and said, "Dude, your painting sucks."

Mitch thought, *A smart ass. Good, just what I need to keep my skills up.* And he replied, "Maybe it sucks because you're in it."

"Ah, that's why it ain't telling me anything." He stuck out his hand. "Call me Surfer."

Mitch shook hands and thought, *I could like this sun-fried, little guy.* "Call me Mitch."

———

At Malibu Seafood Chad had his group gathered together at the rustic tables. After picking up their orders from the service window, Chad announced, "Listen up, everybody. Mitch Alexander joined us this morning. He's an Art Center guy. He cranked out a real winner." Chad held up the wet painting for the group to see and got murmurs of approval.

Surfer exclaimed, "Shit hot, Dude, really awesome!"

"Let's welcome him aboard with a big round of applause."

Clapping, cheers, and whistles came from a dozen classmates.

Chad sat next to Mitch. "I am going to tell you what this kind of art therapy is all about.

"Traditional art therapy serves as a release of dark secrets. It is very introspective, examining, as it does, detritus of earlier traumas and negative influences that come from the mind. That's fine for most people—for a while. Then after they have unloaded a lot of bad karma, they need something more.

"That's where Plein Air Expression comes into play. It opens us up to the world around us. Now a lot of people think: What's the big deal? Everyone likes a beautiful sunset or Niagara Falls. True enough. But while they are seeing beautiful nature, they have not turned off the background noise of everyday life. Plein Air Expression does this—when we get into the zone."

"The zone?" asked Mitch.

Chad continued. "Basically when you paint along the shore, you must concentrate on the ever-changing light and color. You lose yourself in it; it hypnotizes you because it demands the highest level of concentration to capture a scene in about two hours, before the light changes too much. Distracting thoughts are blocked out. Noise too. The uninterrupted impact of natural beauty on the mind for a couple hours is a powerful endorphin pump. This is all good for recovering minds."

———

Two days later Mitch came back to the beach for painting again with Surfer. They picked unsuspecting groups of bathers for subjects and painted quick studies of them. Surfer eyed Mitch's painting, "Awesome job of a gnarly subject, all them kids running around. You're styling, Dude."

Within weeks Mitch grew addicted to painting in the zone. He was oblivious to the world around him, except for the sound of waves and the shapes and colors in front of him—which he raced against the clock to capture. Chad was right on—beach-painting sessions put him in a feel-good state. Left him feeling expansive and happy for two or three days thereafter. No pills needed either.

Between beach days he didn't mind trudging around to find a used car in running condition. He had squirreled away fifteen hundred dollars for the car he would buy sometime in the future. Money from his disability checks. Feeling better after two weeks at the beach, he found the courage to walk to car lots within four miles of the Brewery. Eight miles round trip was doable with all the practice he had since leaving Mount San Gorgonio.

A week's search found the 1990 blue Honda Civic at Flapper Smith's Chevrolet in Boyle Heights. The salesman said it had belonged to an old couple in J-Town who never took it on the freeway. Had 110,000 miles—if you believed Flapper didn't spin back the odometer. Tires OK. Paint faded to blue brown on top, but it ran good, didn't smoke, and had a muffler without holes.

With the car Mitch began hitting Malibu three or four times a week. He always ate lunch at Malibu Seafood with its Styrofoam boxes of delicious food eaten at picnic tables. Funky enough for him to feel comfortable—and he got to know other artists that hung there too.

———

The girls in bikinis started looking good to him again—when he wasn't in the zone.

Chapter 4

PAINTING AT EL PESCADOR

With the blue Honda, Mitch could get out beyond the last bus stop at Trancas Beach. A few more miles up Pacific Coast Highway he came upon three state beaches: El Matador, La Piedra, and El Pescador. Driving around, looking for painting spots, he saw their signs along the highway and checked them out. They all had small gravel parking lots, a slot to drop in an eight-dollar parking fee, and the iconic Porta-Potty.

El Matador was the most spectacular of the three with its high cliffs overlooking massive rock formations in the shallows. Fashion shoots and movie filming were frequent there. El Matador always had the most parked cars and the most foot traffic on its path down to the beach, a hundred feet below.

On this day Mitch was looking for something more tranquil. He drove a mile past El Matador to El Pescador. Just a few cars parked in the lot. Hardly anyone there. Great for quiet reflection.

He walked a hundred yards to the cliff's edge and scouted around to find the best view. "This is it," he said, while looking through his hands held like a viewfinder, framing the cove below. He erected his beat-up French easel, bought for five bucks at the Brewery artist exchange, set an orange-toned canvas on it, and composed his painting with a brush sketch in light blue.

In his reflective mood, he pondered the billions of years of evolution that built the mountains behind him, the cliff he was standing on, the jagged reefs below, and the ocean itself. He thought about how he could sense something that he couldn't define when perceiving nature. It was as if the past had left a fingerprint on the scene he was painting. Some artists called it a "sense of place." Others called it "spiritual vibes." Whatever—it was the secret sauce of existence that instilled energy in a painting—if the artist succeeded in getting a bit of it on the canvas.

He brushed in the curving beach below with its small, white house peeking around the cliff's far end. The house was built well above high-tide level. Its rocky backyard fell off into reefs that slanted downward beneath the surface on a calm day.

After ten minutes or so, Mitch had painted himself out of the reflective mode—and into the zone. There was no thinking about things in the zone, just an unconscious connection of his senses, his instincts, and his brushes.

The cliff face approaching the house at the far end of the cove was mostly covered with gray chaparral. The gray changed, becoming a combination of teal mixed with terra rosa, after he gazed at it intently. Stroking these colors on canvas documented his discovery.

Where not covered by chaparral, the cliff was ocherous red. As the morning mist burned off, the red earth of the cliff revealed more glowing color than at first appeared. Hungrily he captured its glow in the moments before it faded.

He painted waves lapping the beach in shades of warm or cool white—never chalky, straight-out-of-the-tube white. Progressing farther out to sea, he painted hues of cobalt, cerulean, purple, and viridian.

Mitch painted top speed—grabbing values and intensities of color notes—before the light changed.

Offshore the morning mist lifted like a curtain, slowly revealing the horizon. Aquamarine shading of the far ocean darkened in patches where there was a breeze. He grabbed those shapes too and threw them on the canvas.

He left the little house for last, capturing its sun-dappled white sides, overhanging palms, and bougainvillea on the fence with rapid strokes. Then standing back for a last look, he declared the painting finished.

Mitch thought, *I've been in the zone for a couple of hours. Sound of waves lapping on the beach. Feel of the gentle breeze. Painting came together with some secret sauce in it. This is it— as good as it gets. Gotta call Burt to tell him how great painting at the beach has worked out for me.*

Gathering his gear and heading for the parking lot, he realized he was starved. Twenty minutes later found him in line at Malibu Seafood. When he made it in the door and to the cash register, he ordered an ahi burger to be washed down with a bottle of Mango Madness. He exited the banging screen door and was waiting near the pickup window when he heard Surfer shouting, "Hey, Nut Case, we're over here."

Surfer, Chad, and some therapy group members made room for him at a front table—with a primo view of the ocean. Surfer asked, "Where you been hanging at, Dude?"

"El Pescador, on the cliff overlooking the cove toward the west. I call it the Hideaway Cove."

"How'd the painting work out?" asked Chad.

"I think I nailed it today."

"Talk about nailing stuff—you shoulda seen all the gash at the Pier where we were strokin' on the paint," said Surfer.

"Surrrferrrr!" groaned Jeannie, another of the artists in Chad's group—but that didn't dislodge his lecherous grin.

Chad said sternly, "Surfer, knock off the vulgarity."

Jeannie added, "Yeah, gives Plein Air Expression a bad reputation."

Mitch said, "I'm going back to El Pescador every day for a month to paint the Hideaway Cove."

Surfer snorted, "Will that kind of obsessive behavior help the reputation?"

"You never know," said Mitch with a chuckle, "but it might make mine."

"Do tell, Dude," said Surfer sarcastically.

"Painting there every day will get me into the vibes of that cove and the mysterious little, white house at the far end of the beach," said Mitch enthusiastically.

"Boring, Dude—same place every day," said Surfer

"I am going to find a story there if I keep painting it. Like Monet and the haystacks," said Mitch, undeterred.

"That's truth seeking," added Chad intensely. "Go for it man."

———

Mitch returned to El Pescador every day, working at different times to explore the impact of different light angles on the Hideaway Cove scene. On his fifteenth day, Chad and Surfer joined him for painting in the morning and had already gone for lunch. Mitch said he would follow in half an hour.

Earlier they discussed the white house and had agreed it would be a great writer's hideaway. It had everything a writer would need: solitude; distance from distractions; a lonely beach to walk on; and for a change of scenery—a few low-key bars along Pacific Coast Highway. He joked with the guys. "Hell, if I ever move there I'm gonna become a writer."

Now alone, concentrating on capturing the house on canvas, Mitch said, to no one in particular, "There is someone moving behind the curtains. Can't tell for sure. Maybe my eyes are playing tricks on me. Never seen anyone outside— just pelicans or seagulls roosting on the rocks."

Chapter 5

IN THE CROSSHAIRS

Inside the little, white house at the end of the cove, it was anything but a writer's hideaway. Fidel Terrasombra, brother of El Jefe, the feared Mexican drug cartel boss, and Javier Espinosa, a cartel soldier, were arguing about the artist on the high ground above the cove. Javier had opened a kitchen window enough to get a clear shot with his rifle. He saw the artist through the scope—even the expression on his face. The artist seemed to be talking to himself. With Mitch's head in the crosshairs, Javier said, "I could take him out now, Fidel."

"You loco? Put that gun down."

Javier put it on the table and groused, "No painter with *cojones* needs two weeks for the little picture he is doing."

"You shoot him with people around," said Fidel in a loud voice. "They call the cops. Cops will know where the shot came from."

Javier came up with another idea. "Why don't you go up there and phone me when no one's around."

"And then?"

"I shoot him, and you roll his body over the cliff."

Fidel, now exasperated, said, "We must use our heads with this guy. He might really be an artist."

"He's here every day—up there looking down at us. That's trouble."

"Maybe not," said Fidel thoughtfully, looking out the window at Mitch painting above. "We don't want no unnecessary attention."

"What are you going to do about him?"

"First I'll see if he knows how to paint."

"I think he is working with the cops. Lemme take the shot."

"Relax, Javier," said Fidel firmly. "That's an order."

"*Sí*, Fidel." Javier sighed in resignation.

"I am going up to talk with our artist," said Fidel, as he finished his beer and set the glass on the counter.

"You're going to let him see you came from here?"

"No. I'll be driving out the back way to the highway." Fidel picked up his keys. "I drive down to the parking lot. Walking to the cliff from the parking lot, the artist won't know I came from down here."

"Be cool, Fidel."

"Don't worry. I got some ideas to fix this problem."

———

Mitch jumped when a stranger said, "Hello, Amigo," startling him out of the zone.

Seeing the stranger's cowboy hat and boots, Mitch replied, "Howdy, Partner," still stroking on paint and hoping the guy would keep walking.

No dice. He just stood there watching.

Finally the stranger said, "How long does it take to paint a picture?"

"An hour or two—if not disturbed," said Mitch.

"Could you paint a portrait of me?"

"Yeah, but it will cost you."

"I'll give you a hundred bucks," said the stranger in a friendly way.

Mitch thought, *I need cash, but I do have my standards.* "Let's make it two hundred, and I'll paint you in an hour."

"OK, Amigo. You got a deal," said the stranger. "When can you do it?"

"After lunch. Two o'clock."

"No problem. See you at two," said the stranger and walked off toward the parking lot.

Chapter 6

PAINTING FIDEL

Minutes later Mitch drove to Malibu Seafood to meet Chad and Surfer.

"Guys, I just got a commission to paint a portrait," said Mitch as he sat down with them.

Surfer quipped, "Got your crayons?"

Mitch laughed and replied, "Jealousy brings out the worst in you, Surfer."

Chad asked, "How'd it happen, Mitch?"

"A guy comes along while I was painting. Watches me for a while and then asks if I could paint him."

Surfer snapped, "He saw your painting and still wanted you to paint him?"

"Surfer, this man's got taste. Looks like he's got cash too," said Mitch. "I told him I could do his portrait in an hour."

"Wow! *This* I must see," said Chad in amazement.

"I'm painting him at two o'clock," said Mitch, "at the Hideaway Cove overlook."

"Dude, if you're done in an hour and that sucker buys it, lunch tomorrow is on me," said Surfer with a smirk.

———

Mitch returned to his morning painting spot. Waiting there—the stranger.

"Right on time," he said with a smile.

"Hate to keep an art lover waiting," joked Mitch.

"Where do I stand?" asked the stranger.

"You'll be sitting. Easier to hold steady that way."

"As you like, Amigo."

"I want you to sit on the picnic table with your feet on the bench." Mitch set up his easel six feet away, facing the stranger sitting on the table. After toning his canvas with a warm gray wash to cover the glaring white surface, Mitch told the stranger he was ready to roll and to stay as still as possible in his pose. They were quiet. With only the whisper of the brush on canvas to be heard, he sketched in facial features, hat, shoulders, and shirt collar.

Mitch painted with quick strokes. His wide brush covered the canvas in ten minutes with large areas of thin paint. Basic shapes were accurately established. Then, covering the darkest areas first—hat, shadow under chin, and eyes—he eased into the zone. But this wasn't the mellow zone of beach painting. This was the unblinking eyeball-to-eyeball zone.

Is this guy mad dogging me? wondered Mitch. *Is that gaze fixed on my eyes a malevolent stare of a gangbanger?* He looked back and forth from easel to subject—locking in for moments at the stranger's menacing dark eyes while scanning facial hills and valleys.

Mitch ignored the eyes by focusing on the bridge of the nose, and kept painting. He worked big areas with his usual rich colors, then smaller areas, refining features, and adjusting lights and darks of hair and shirt.

Halfway into it, Chad and Surfer sauntered up. They were talking and laughing.

The stranger asked, "Who are they?"

"Artist friends of mine."

"You guys paint here a lot?"

"Yeah, we paint Malibu all the time," said Mitch without stopping. "I've been painting the cove down there every day."

"Why every day?"

"Sometimes I paint the same subject over and over," Mitch said. "Gives me insight into what's going on."

"Hmmm…when you going to stop painting it?" asked the stranger.

"Don't know…a week or two, I guess. When there's nothing more to learn."

"Paint and learn, eh?"

"Yeah, right now I am wondering about the little house. Don't know who lives there, if anyone." Painting rapidly he continued, "I could imagine myself living there, writing a novel. Away from the distractions of the city."

"Yeah, hadn't thought of that," said the stranger without changing expression.

Still painting, Mitch continued, "It's almost completely isolated. From down on the beach, no other house can be seen in either direction."

Mitch raced on, lathering rich, thick strokes to refine passages on face and hat, and headed for the finish line.

Chad and Surfer watched from a few feet back to give him room. No one talked as the hour's end neared.

Sitting still for a long time caused the stranger to squirm and his features to move a bit—hints to be captured with the flick of a brush, hints that revealed facets of a man about whom Mitch knew nothing an hour ago.

Mitch thought, *This is a tough guy with a hard stare. Wouldn't want to cross him.*

He painted the final deft strokes on facial highlights and then took a step back to scan for areas that still needed adjustment. Couldn't find any. With a theatrical flourish, Mitch announced, "Ta Daaah! Painting is finished, Señor."

The stranger got up stiffly. He stretched, studied the painting for some moments, and smiled faintly. "You're very talented," he said and kept looking at the painting while nodding his head slightly up and down. "*Muy talentoso.*"

Chad came closer to take a look. "Damn good portrait—done in an hour."

Mitch added his signature at the bottom left corner, took it off the easel, and handed it to the stranger.

"Thanks, Amigo," said the stranger, giving Mitch two crisp hundreds and disappearing up the path to the parking lot. His car was heard starting and crunching gravel as it drove on to the highway.

Surfer looked disappointed. "Lunch on me, Dude, when I see you again."

Mitch threw his arm around Surfer's shoulders. "Surfer, old buddy, you'll see me tomorrow at Malibu Seafood." He grinned and added, "Lobster, three-pounder—market price, baked potato, cole slaw, couple of beers."

"Cryzus Jeast, Dude. Got me on the mat, and you're jumping up and down on me."

With his arm still around Surfer's shoulders, Mitch said, "Let's shoot for twelve sharp."

Chapter 7

EL JEFE

Maximilliano Terrasombra, known as El Jefe, built his main hacienda deep in the heart of Michoacán. Called El Mirador, it was situated like all his homes, at the end of a long, unpaved road from a main highway. It benefited from natural landscape features that would allow for defense in case of attack from just about any threat—even the Mexican Army. Walls of the hacienda stood twelve-feet high and were topped with broken glass. Three armed men guarded the entrance gate at all times.

Marta Ordoñez drove up to the gate and stopped while her trunk and car interior were checked. Then she was let in to park in one of the spaces for couriers. Like El Jefe's other couriers, she enjoyed coming to El Mirador. She could eat delicious food, swim in a pool, and take a nap before driving home. Best of all, she was provided a reliable car, and paid generously in cash with each delivery.

Also at El Mirador was Raul Casteneda. Raul had been El Jefe's chief of south Michoacán operations for the past five years. He was used to operating independently and had a separate methamphetamine operation of his own. El Jefe tolerated it until now because of Raul's value to the cartel. Tough and good-looking, he was ruthlessly effective in his management of cartel operations, and he reminded El Jefe of himself twenty years earlier.

El Jefe needed a lieutenant to work closely with him to handle expanding business. He was bringing Raul along, hoping that there could be a fit. Raul dressed conservatively, usually in suits, and was not into flashy jewelry and tattoos. He looked like a prosperous businessman. El Jefe liked that style and increasingly included Raul in top-level assignments.

El Jefe's brother, Fidel, had no interest in being tied down to the home operation. He liked the role of troubleshooter with no regular responsibilities and didn't have any problems with Raul's rise to the top level. The other logical choice for lieutenant was El Jefe's oldest son, Jorge. But he was only fourteen and lived with his mother and other siblings in Aspen. El Jefe doubted he would ever fit in like a Michoacán-raised muchacho.

Marta Ordoñez brought messages she had downloaded from a Guanajuato Internet café on a thumb drive—including Mitch's portrait of Fidel. El Jefe opened it on his office computer. He knew immediately he had his artist.

"Raul," he called, "come here."

Raul, who had been smoking a cigar and practicing billiards in the adjacent room, responded, "Sí, Jefe." He strolled into El Jefe's office and sat down in a leather chair near the desk.

Swiveling his chair to face Raul, El Jefe said, "I have a job for you that must be done right, from beginning to end. I want Fidel to grab the artist that painted this picture in California. Then bring him here by our submarine."

"*Por qué*, Jefe?" Raul exhaled cigar smoke.

"He will paint a portrait of mi madre."

"Very well, Jefe, I will tell Marta to send Fidel that order from an Internet café."

There was no telephone, cell phone, or Internet service at El Jefe's houses. He had couriers like Marta using Internet cafés or cell phones at least fifty kilometers from his houses to communicate with the outside world.

"Raul, when the *artista* arrives, take him from the submarine to my hacienda near San Miguel de Allende," said El Jefe while lighting a cigar.

"Sí, Jefe."

"He will be a prisoner—but we will treat him very kindly. I want you to ensure he feels welcome, from the minute he arrives until you deliver him to the hacienda."

"Make him feel welcome, Jefe?" asked Raul with raised eyebrows, looking surprised.

"He has to think he is a guest and will be set free when the portrait is finished. Mi madre must believe the artist is a guest too. At the hacienda I have a man named Panchito who will keep him happy.

"And after that?"

"Raul, you and Hector are going to kill him. The artist will know too much about our operation by the time he finishes the portrait. He will know about the submarine and about my hacienda near San Miguel."

"It will be done, Jefe."

———

Horses were brought up to the main house. El Jefe and Raul mounted and trotted off. El Jefe was proud of his fields under cultivation that were interwoven with picturesque arroyos and stands of trees. He pointed out areas of great beauty— especially with the setting sun—and described varieties of grapes growing in his vineyard.

At the high ground of the vineyard stood the winery. El Jefe and Raul dismounted there and went inside. El Jefe gave Raul a tour, accompanied by the cellar master. They then talked privately in the tasting room.

"Raul, I am glad you are here tonight. You are a stand-up guy in our organization. You have what it takes to fight off our enemies and to grow our operation. But I must ask one thing of you. I do not want members of my organization to have their own businesses on the side."

"I understand your concern, Jefe."

"It will be best for us to put your operation under my management—don't worry about your income. It won't be decreased—it will be increased."

"Thank you, Jefe," said Raul who was appreciating the heavy wood design of the winery. "I admire the way you get things done and will bring my chemical operation under the umbrella of your power."

"Let me tell you a little more about how I operate. Loyalty is número uno in my empire. It is well rewarded and violations of it are fatal."

"As is should be, Jefe," said Raul, realizing now he was being groomed to enter the highest level of power with El Jefe.

El Jefe continued. "I am extremely secretive about family matters. No one talks to newspapers or has Internet connections. My wife and children live in Aspen most of the year under a different name. I visit them on a random basis so my travels cannot be anticipated. My family believes I am in the export-import business.

"I encourage you to buy into legal businesses and observe all business laws. This way we blend into powerful circles more easily.

"To many, I am just another billionaire. My legitimate businesses are well known. Because billionaires in Mexico live private lives in walled compounds, I don't stand out from that crowd. Like them I have a number of houses in Mexico, but unlike them I use them on a random basis to keep my enemies guessing about where I am."

Raul agreed. "Makes sense, Jefe. Discretion is key to security."

———

The two men walked to the winery patio where El Jefe continued. "I have a niece, Amparo Terrasombra—most attractive. After our artist disappears, I will introduce you two. Until now I have scared away any man interested in her. But I won't scare you away. A marriage between you and Amparo would be a further cementing of our relationship and blending of our operations."

This turn of conversation surprised Raul. "Jefe, I am still single and had assumed that I would find my own wife."

El Jefe said, "This is all months away. I do not insist you marry her, and she doesn't know of you—yet. But if you two have an interest in each other, you have my blessing."

Raul said, "I look forward to meeting more of your family—especially the good looking ones."

They laughed, and El Jefe raised his glass. "*Salud,* Amigo."

As they talked the chef removed a suckling pig from the outdoor barbeque and took it into the winery kitchen for carving. A table was set for four on the patio, and torches were lit.

Two sexy girls in their twenties drove up in a golf cart. El Jefe introduced Raul to Esmeralda Lopez. "She's your party doll, Raul, enjoy the evening." El Jefe then put his arm around the other girl and said, "Flor Diaz is my date. Now, let us sit down for dinner."

El Jefe proposed a toast: "Salud and good appetite." They raised their glasses, and as they sipped their wine three musicians joined a guitarist, who had been playing softly in the shadows. The tempo picked up, and a sumptuous dinner was served. Wine flowed freely. Lively voices and laughter floated into the night.

A jovial El Jefe admitted that at one time he wanted to be an artist. Flor teased, "Don't give up your regular job just yet."

El Jefe laughed. "No chance of that. Back then the taunts of other teenagers about my art angered me. I attacked those who tried to bully me with fists and feet.

"In time I got to love beating up other kids more than studying art—and my life went in another direction." Everyone laughed. "No more fists and feet, you understand. I switched to more serious armament." He pulled out a semi-automatic pistol and fired three shots into a starry night to make his point.

Everyone sobered for a moment—always happens when someone pulls out a gun—and then the laughter resumed. El Jefe put the gun back in its shoulder holster and looked into Raul's eyes. "I have no regrets. My love for aggression and power brought me all this," he said with a sweeping gesture.

Flor said, "You got any regrets about me, Maxi?"

"Not so far, Flor, *mi cariño*. Just keep me happy—and stay out of sight."

Turning back to Raul, El Jefe said, "Amigo, you will enjoy life in the Terrasombra family."

Raul, who had an arm around Esmeralda's shoulders, said, "I already am."

Chapter 8

HIDEAWAY VISIT

"Oh, good Jesus, the nightmares are back," moaned Mitch, going in and out of sleep. *Real dark. Can't move around much. Have I died? Droning noise. Is it a motor? Or a nightmare buzz?* He struggled to comprehend. *Feels like I'm in a boat.*

He dozed off seconds, maybe longer. Came back to the same droning noise. Like a diesel. His thoughts were rising through a haze: *I'm awake lying in some kind of bunk. What's this? Shit, got something on my ankle. Can move my leg, but can't shake it off. Heavy. Some kind of metal ring. Be tough to walk with that on. Can't make out much in the dim light. Sounds like water... against a boat's hull...*

Then a terrifying realization!

It's not a nightmare. It's the real thing.

He wondered, *How'd I get here? I feel dopey—like when I came to after the operation in Afghanistan. Dreamy sort of....*

———

A memory unfurled from the fog of semiconsciousness: Painting at the usual spot on El Pescador cliff, Mitch saw a man leaving the little, white house and walking along Hideaway Cove beach in his direction. Disappeared from view beneath the edge of the cliff, then minutes later, the man reappeared, making his way up the trail from the beach.

At the top, a hundred yards away, Mitch recognized him. *Same guy I painted yesterday. Weird. Didn't say he lived in the Hideaway Cove house. Maybe yesterday he didn't want me to know. He's headed this way.*

Mitch remembered that the guy was friendlier this time. He smiled, great teeth, and said, "Hey, your picture, she is a knockout."

"Thanks. Uh…"

"I am Fidel," the man said and they shook hands.

"I'm Mitch. Good to meet you."

"Mitch, I invite you down to my house," said Fidel exuberantly.

"The white house down there?" Mitch remembered asking, pointing down toward the Hideaway Cove.

"That's it," said Fidel. "You said you wanted to know more about it."

Mitch remembered that he had said, "That's totally cool of you, man."

"After that super painting, it is the least I can do," said Fidel.

"Been wondering for two weeks what it would be like to live there."

"Come on down and see for yourself."

Mitch remembered walking down to the beach. Left his painting gear at the top. Not worried about getting ripped off. No one touches an artist's half-finished work on a funky, old easel.

Plodding through the beach sand, they came to stone steps behind the house. As they approached the backdoor, Mitch remembered it was opened from inside by another Latino guy—buffed out, tattooed. He said, "*Pase*," smiled his set of great teeth, and introduced himself as Javier.

"I'm Mitch." Powerful handshake.

They walked into a modern kitchen.

"Got a cold beer for you, Mitch."

"Thanks, man." Mitch remembered the big slug of Dos Equis Dark. I needed something cold after slogging down the path and through the soft beach sand. "This beer has a real different taste."

"Sí, Mitch, it's for those who love beer with a lot of body. Staying for lunch?"

"Can't, Javier, meeting artist friends at Malibu Seafood."

"Ah so. Too bad," said Javier, looking disappointed.

"I won a bet that I couldn't paint Fidel in an hour. Now I am going to collect my free lunch." Mitch remembered saying that—but didn't remember meeting the guys for lunch.

"I understand, but let us show you around before you go."

Mitch didn't remember much more. They took a tour of the rooms, everything in good condition. They showed him the garage with Jet Skis and a Zodiac in it. A back door and ramp to the water made for easy launching. He remembered thinking, *I could live here and be happy.*

Back at the kitchen counter talking, Mitch had a vague recollection of Fidel and Javier telling him how nights were especially dark with no city or other house lights in view. Mitch was thinking it was perfect solitude for a writer—or even for an artist.

Mitch started gulping down another Dos Equis, with that rusty-old-nails taste. Had to drink up to keep his lunch date with Surfer. Recalled beer hitting him fast…

Mitch thought, *Room starting to spin, two of them watching, then holding me as I had trouble standing. Voices drifting farther away…lying on the floor—and then…*

…Here, on a boat!

Chapter 9

SUBMARINE

Mitch was dropping in and out of sleep. A man appeared in the dim light at the end of the compartment. He came closer, bent down, looked to see if Mitch's eyes were open.

"Welcome aboard, Artista. Can you hear me OK?"

"Yeah, great," croaked Mitch, still feeling dopey, like being drunk. Too dark to clearly see whose face it was above him. He saw he was in a boat compartment. Damn small—just room for a couple of bunks and a crapper.

"This is probably your first submarine ride," said the man looking down at him.

Panic surged from the depths of Mitch's very being. He remembered sneaking through tunnels in Afghanistan, searching for an enemy that could be around every curve. Way under the earth with no easy way out. Trembling violently, he screamed, "Submarine! Under water! Get me the fuck outta here!"

He struggled to rise from…something was holding him down. Screams were still bursting from his lungs. Other men appeared in the gloom to hold his arms and legs still. One of them gave him an injection to stop his screaming—he sank into unconsciousness.

———

When he woke warm, humid air was blowing through the compartment. The sound of waves slapping against the hull told him they were cruising on the surface. The air was fresh with the scent of the shore mixed with the smell of the Pacific, and it cleared his head enough for him to sit up.

Crewmembers unlocked the leg iron and helped him up. Javier took him above to the conning tower, where he saw Mexico's coast two miles to port.

"How did I get here?" asked Mitch, while holding on to the railing for support against the wind and rolling swells.

Javier answered, "You are about to have the best art commission of your life. You will be painting El Jefe's mother."

"El Jefe. Who?" asked Mitch, struggling to understand.

"A powerful man, maybe the most powerful in Mexico. What he wants, Amigo—he gets. We suggest you paint this portrait of La Señora. It is very important to him. If you do exactly as El Jefe says, you will be treated well. Don't cross El Jefe. You risk your life—family and friends lives too—if you fuck with him."

The captain, with a northern-European accent, said, "Take him out on rear deck. Hose him down; he stinks."

————

Three hours later, the sub entered a small harbor. Javier told him it was Puerto Rana Verde and it was located on the Mexican mainland, below the end of Baja. Not much about the harbor registered with him except that it had a tropical, sinister look and humidity to match. Awake but still groggy from the injections, Mitch was hustled ashore and put into a black Ford Explorer—back seat, next to Javier.

Itzak at the wheel drove fast but skillfully through verdant hills east of Puerto Rana Verde. Raul, in the front right seat, was obviously in charge. They stopped at a small hotel where Raul turned to him and said, "Mitch, we're cleaning you up."

"Another saltwater hose down?"

"A ha ha!" Raul laughed. "We had to do that because you were smelling pretty—how you say, ripe."

"Steam cleaning this time?"

"You are going to the spa here—yes sir, they have a steam room," Raul said with a grin. "Two ladies are going to give you a shave, haircut, and massage after your steam."

"*Muchas gracias,* Raul. This trip keeps gettin' better."

Javier bought him denim pants and a shirt, woven sandals called *huaraches*, and underwear in the market by the hotel. The steam room sweated out more of the dopey feeling, and the massage and shave had him feeling good but damn hungry. After putting on his new clothes, he wolfed down a pair of fish tacos, which made him feel a hell-of-a-lot better. He was still scared—but he vowed not to let those assholes know it.

Two hours after stopping, they were on the road again. Raul, explained things: "You are here to paint a portrait of El Jefe's mother, La Señora. Based on the portrait you did of Fidel, El Jefe picked you for the job. Do not attempt to leave before it's done, or we'll find you. We'll kill you. You'll be living in a beautiful hacienda—treated well while you paint La Señora. Do not tell anyone how you got there. Anybody asks, tell them you are the guest artist. When finished, you get paid a lot of money and go home."

"I understand," said Mitch—not sure he did understand.

A couple of stops to stretch their legs, eat tacos, and dig into their cooler of beer had gone a long way to disperse the strained atmosphere they started with. Finally Mitch blurted out, "Why me to paint a picture of El Jefe's mom? Why not get a Mexican painter?"

Itzak said, "Mexican artists know about El Jefe; they get too nervous to paint La Señora."

"Well fuck me—I'll never smile again!" said Mitch looking away at the sunset's purple shadows.

Laughs all around. Raul commented, "That's real funny, Mitch."

"Yeah, like a rubber crutch," said Mitch, unable to hide the sarcasm.

The explorer wound its way relentlessly across the great plateau of central Mexico. Behind them a red sun disappeared.

Painting El Jefe's mother, Mitch mused, *could be a new beginning—or a new ending. Either way, I'm gonna paint real slow.*

Chapter 10

BAFFLED

The day after Mitch's disappearance, police were at El Pescador State Beach collecting evidence, photographing the scene, and questioning anyone who had been in contact with him. A circle of yellow tape surrounded his easel and the backpack lying near it.

Chad and Surfer had been questioned separately in the morning. In the afternoon they were still hanging around, wishing they could contribute something more.

A reporter found them. "Fellas, can you tell us what Mitch was doing yesterday?"

Chad explained, "We were going to meet Mitch for lunch at Malibu Seafood. He had been here a lot lately, doing a series on the cove down there. His painting gear is still here."

The reporter looked up from his note pad. "Anything you can tell from looking at his equipment?"

"Looks like he took a break and planned to come back—because everything is still out. His brushes aren't cleaned.

Like he meant to be away from his easel for a short time, come back, and finish his painting. It's just half finished," said Chad, pointing at the work in progress.

The reporter said, "When did you guys get suspicious something was wrong?"

Surfer said, "When Mitch didn't show for lunch we came here. His car was still parked over there. Where it still is. At sunset when he still didn't show up we called Malibu PD."

"What's his full name?"

"Mitchell Alexander," said Surfer.

"Can you tell us any more about him? Where did Mitch live? Why was he painting here?"

Chad said, "Lived in downtown LA at the Brewery Lofts. He started coming out to paint along the coast three or four months ago. He was in my Plein Air Expression therapy workshop and had made tremendous progress in his struggle against PTSD."

"What branch of the military did he serve in?"

Chad responded, "Mitch saw action in Afghanistan with the marines. Left him traumatized. He was functioning at a near-normal level in recent months. Had everything to live for."

Surfer added, "We've been passing out flyers to the artists, surfers, tourists—anyone we can give one to."

The flyer was a grainy picture of Mitch at Malibu Seafood. It read: "If you have seen this man, call Malibu PD. He is about 6-feet tall, 30 to 35-years-old, dressed in denim shirt and pants. Medium-thin build, about 160 pounds. Dark blond hair, brown eyes."

The reporter asked, "Had you guys seen anything unusual before he disappeared?"

Chad said, "Day before yesterday a man approached him and asked him to paint his portrait. I'll show you on my iPhone." He took out his iPhone and showed the snapshots of Mitch painting Fidel.

Lieutenant Bailey from Malibu PD appeared. The reporter asked him if there were any new developments.

The lieutenant responded, "We don't have much to add from our morning statements to you all. We have divers scouring the ocean bottom for a mile in each direction. Gone house-to-house questioning residents. Come up with nothing so far."

"FBI on this case?" asks another reporter.

"Not yet. Following a disappearance incident, if we have no solution in one week we call in the FBI to investigate. They handle possible kidnappings."

Chapter II

THE HACIENDA

After traveling many miles across central Mexico's lonely plateau, Mitch was on the downhill side of a beer-and-tequila buzz. Conversation with the three muchachos had ceased. The sun had dropped below a purple horizon, and sunset colors morphed to royal blue.

Mitch thought these wide-open spaces were like the ocean in a way. Same feeling of great distance and wonderment. *I'll paint it someday—if I get out of here alive.*

As darkness fell, he nodded off to sleep and then was jolted awake as the Explorer bumped onto a gravel road. After twenty minutes of rough riding, they arrived at the gate of a walled hacienda. They were waved in by an armed guard and parked in the central courtyard.

"*Hola,* Artista, I'm Panchito," said a jovial man with a white walrus mustache, in heavily accented English. "This way to your adobe. I think you will like it."

They headed away from the courtyard parking area toward an adobe building about a hundred-feet away in the front, left corner of the walls.

"Sure beats submarine living," said Mitch, eying the adobe interior with its arched *boveda* ceilings, white stucco walls, and fireplace. Everything was first class. The planked floor looked newly waxed. The bed was antique vintage, but its spread and pillows were designer chic.

"Heh, heh. Heard you was a joker. You got three nice rooms, Amigo—studio here in front, bedroom, and bathroom. We will bring food to you from the main kitchen any time you want. There is everything you need to paint La Señora." He pointed to an easel with a three-by-four-foot canvas on it.

Great, Mitch thought, *it will take a long time to cover that!* A worktable was laden with expensive oils, brushes, medium, and even a mahl stick for steadying his hand.

"Señorita Amparo picked out the art stuff in Mexico City," said Panchito, noticing Mitch was looking over the neatly arranged tubes, brushes, and cans of medium and thinner.

"Señorita Amparo?" asked Mitch, still reading the names on the paint tubes.

"Sí a niece of El Jefe. Very beautiful. Owns a big gallery in Mexico City, San Ángel district."

"Best-quality art supplies—I'm impressed with Señorita Amparo."

"Don't get too impressed," said Panchito, looking directly at Mitch, without a hint of his earlier joviality. "El Jefe don't want no one near her. He don't want no man alone with her either."

"OK, Panchito. I'll stick to the painting."

"That's it, Mitch. El Jefe wants you to be happy here. There is shaving stuff and clothes for you in the bedroom—even pajamas."

"*Muy amable,*" said Mitch. "That's very nice of you."

"Ah, you speak Spanish?"

"*Poquito*, from high school."

"OK, I bring dinner," said Panchito as he walked off toward the main house.

Twenty minutes later Panchito and the chef brought trays of food. They set up places for two on a patio table. The patio, like the studio, was beautiful. Its Talavera floor tiles, open beams with retractable sunshade, and giant terra-cotta pots, overflowing with bougainvillea, revealed the touch of a professional designer.

Mitch sat down with Panchito to *enchiladas de carnitas* and all the trimmings. *Food couldn't be any better,* he thought, after a few bites.

It was pleasant eating with just candles for illumination. Panchito described the hacienda's main features: The central house had eight bedrooms, a large dining room, commercial style kitchen, and game room. There were other adobes for the staff diagonally across the compound. There was also a small chapel for La Señora. Laurel and oak trees added a romantic, old Mexico feel to the walled-in complex. From what he could see at night, everything appeared well cared for.

Mitch asked if the hacienda was El Jefe's home.

Panchito said, "El Jefe has several homes in Michoacán that he spends most of his time in. He bought this hacienda for his parents years ago and fixed it up. His father died about five years ago, so today it is the home of his mother, La Señora. El Jefe doesn't come here often, and usually it is a surprise when he visits. But I do know he is coming tomorrow to welcome you. I…uh…gotta tell you about the chain."

"Chain?"

"Sí, each night we have to put a leg iron and chain on you so you don't escape. The chain is long enough to let you get around your studio and to the bathroom. This way you get privacy because we don't put no guard with you at night."

"I appreciate your concern, Panchito," said Mitch jokingly, but inside his heart sank. The chain sent a grim message.

After dinner and changing into his new pajamas, Panchito affixed the leg-iron around Mitch's ankle and locked it. When Panchito left, Mitch puttered around dragging his chain, just to check things out.

Painting supplies looked good. He found thirteen colors he usually painted with among the boxes of oils. He satisfied himself that everything else needed to paint a large portrait was there.

He found some paperbacks to read. Taking a dog-eared copy of *Under the Volcano*, he flopped onto the bed and read until sleep took over.

Hours later a nightmare about drowning in a leaking submarine had him gasping for breath, throat paralyzed, unable to scream. Got out of bed covered with sweat. Finally, after stumbling around dragging his chain for an eternity, he found a light switch on the wall—and again became the crazed painter of Dream Wrecks.

With trembling hands he squeezed out a ton of oils on the new palette and slathered La Señora's canvas with a torrent of violent color.

He covered the big canvas in three hours, then collapsed into a chair as morning light began to strengthen—and nodded off into deep sleep.

Chapter 12

SAN MIGUEL DE ALLENDE

"Jesus, Gringo, you nuts or something?" yelled El Jefe. "You really fucked up mi madre's canvas."

Mitch woke up with a start, realizing that El Jefe had arrived. An abashed Panchito, carrying a tray of breakfast for him, said, "Mitch, meet El Jefe."

Mitch, still struggling to wake up, got out of his chair. He said, "Nice to meet you, Jefe," and offered his hand. "Sorry about the canvas, but you see I got a problem, a mental problem. Gonna tell you upfront, I get bad nightmares and depression." Noting a darkening expression on El Jefe's face, he added, "But it's not a big deal. If I get right outta bed after a nightmare and paint a picture, I get it out of my system."

El Jefe, with gaze fixed on Mitch's eyes, said, "You are nuts."

"Yeah, told you I got problems—but once I paint a quick abstract, I am A-OK for the rest of the day. I can paint La Señora, no problema. I just need another canvas for her portrait and another fifty or sixty canvases to hold me over for two months of morning paintings while I am doing it."

El Jefe contemplated him in silence for a few moments longer, turned to Panchito, and said, "Take him in to San Miguel and get him whatever he wants."

He turned back to Mitch. "I know you can capture the soul in your paintings—you did it in my brother's painting. You got his good; you got his evil. I know you can capture mi madre's heart and soul. That's why you are here."

El Jefe's attempt to be friendly didn't fit his swagger and fearsome gaze as he said, "I will make your stay enjoyable. Sorry about the leg iron, but I don't want you getting nervous and running away like other *artistas* I had here. When you are done, I will pay you fifty thousand dollars, then put you on an airplane for LA."

"Jefe, I'm your guy. Got some neurosis, but I function normally." Trying not to sound fawning, Mitch said matter-of-factly, "You will be well pleased with La Señora's painting." He noted El Jefe had the same hard eyes as his brother Fidel.

To Panchito, El Jefe said in Spanish, "Take Hector with you to keep an eye on him in town." Then he left.

Panchito unlocked the leg iron. "Eat breakfast, Mitch. Get dressed and we go."

———

Driving to San Miguel, there wasn't much talking with Panchito and Hector. That was fine. *I'm busy,* thought Mitch, *wondering how the sky can be so blue, air so clear, distances so far to the mountains? Must be the high altitude.*

He thought, *I gotta paint this. I love this feeling of space. It will charge my batteries again, just like when I started painting in Malibu.*

San Miguel greeted him with church bells ringing and roosters still crowing at a late-morning hour. Bumping along cobblestone streets to the center of town, Mitch was enthralled by a vibrant tempo of life. Color everywhere—people, balloon hawkers, ice cream wagon in *El Jardín*, as the central plaza is called, and, rising above all, the magnificent La Paroquia, a gothic church of pink limestone.

At the art supply store, *El Gato—Materiales Artisticos,* their order for sixty canvases was too much to handle. The owner said, "Señor, I can give you the thirty-by-forty canvas today, also twenty medium-size canvases. I need two weeks to get forty more medium canvases."

"That's OK. We'll come back in two weeks," Mitch replied, glad for another chance to get away from the hacienda. They loaded canvases, boxes of paints, bottles of painting medium, and brushes into the Explorer and then rumbled over more cobblestones to La Capilla restaurant.

"Best place in town," said Panchito.

At a rooftop table, their lazy afternoon began with Panchito ordering a bottle of tequila and two glasses—he told Hector he had to stay sober to drive home. To Mitch it looked like Panchito was in charge.

Mitch looked out across many rooftops toward the valley below and faraway mountain silhouettes beyond the valley.

He was buzzed now from the tequila and appetizers and he wondered how one could be kidnapped and live so well. Am I getting Stockholm syndrome?

Panchito asked in a kindly way, "Why do you paint those crazy abstracts in the morning?"

"It's from the war. I came back with nightmares, depression, stuff like that," said Mitch between bites of an excellent dinner.

"Painting *abstractos* helps?"

"Yeah, I look a nightmare right in its face and show it on canvas for what it is," said Mitch before a long sip of tequila.

"*Qué interesante.*"

Mitch said, "Gets me through the day. Keeps me normal until the next night."

Mitch again looked out at the distant valley backstopped with towering clouds. Beauty and sadness came in and out of focus along with Panchito's friendly chatter. He could be happy here in Mexico—maybe not forever, but for time to let the immense vistas infuse his canvases with that thread of joy he needs in his life. He needed something to lift him out of the Dream Wreck world again.

Would he get the chance after La Señora's painting is finished? Would these guys who have kidnapped him, chained him to a bed, made him paint their mother—just let him go? He couldn't get those thoughts out of his mind.

Finally Mitch and Panchito, both a little unsteady, and a steadier Hector walked down the restaurant's stone stairs and out the front door to the Explorer. Hector drove out of town. As they traversed the long stretches of highway to the hacienda turnoff, Mitch and Panchito fell asleep. It was after dark when they pulled through the hacienda gate. Still half asleep, they stacked the trove of supplies in the studio.

Mitch prepared for another night chained to the bed and the nightmare just a few hours away.

Chapter 13

FIRST SESSION

Mitch got up well before light to confront his night demons. He painted a Dream Wreck in his usual mad way. Charging the canvas and attacking it with both ends of the brush, palette knives, fingers, and anything else within reach that could make an imprint in oils.

Chain dragging was a big time irritant, but his determination to finish the day's Dream Wreck squelched any desire to quit before Panchito would come to unlock him.

He got it done before Panchito showed up. Felt good about that. *Now these guys will believe that I am OK after finishing my morning Dream Wreck.*

The two ate a hearty breakfast out on the patio, during which he was told that La Señora would visit him at ten o'clock, after mass.

"I want you to look good. Studio too must look good," said Panchito. "El Jefe loves his mother above all. You must respect that love with your best behavior whenever she is here. You and she have to be happy to have it work out good."

"I'm putting a picture of *La Virgen de Guadalupe* in the studio because La Señora is very religious. And finally, Mitch, no talking about submarines or leg chains—you are a guest here."

"I'll be a true *caballero*," said Mitch, watching Panchito holding the picture and searching for the right spot to hang it. "You have my word."

"*Bueno*," said Panchito, satisfied he found the right spot and leaned the picture against the wall below it. "I hang the picture here so La Señora will see it when she walks in the door."

Panchito hammered a nail into the wall and hung the Guadalupe picture. He pushed Mitch's chain under his bed, well out of sight, and straightened things out. He turned the two Dream Wreck paintings to face the wall, looked around the studio carefully, and was satisfied. "See you at ten o'clock."

"See you at ten."

———

When Mitch saw La Señora and Panchito approaching, he went outside to greet them. La Señora was wearing a black lace *mantilla* that draped lightly to her shoulders. Mitch said to himself, *I am going to like La Señora,—whether I like her or not.*

In her late sixties, her face and figure had been treated well by time. He wondered how a woman, with such an angelic appearance, could be the mother of a prick like El Jefe. Her face, framed by wavy, white hair, spoke wisdom. It spoke compassion, but also awareness. Mitch had the feeling that she was no dummy.

Panchito presented Mitch to her. Mitch shook her hand, saying, "Con mucho gusto, Señora Terrasombra."

"*Encantada,* Señor Mitch Alexander."

He invited her into the studio and asked that she sit in the elegant chair Panchito carried in the day before. Light from the front windows illuminated the left side of her face. *Good,* he thought, *those subtle shadows delineate her features.* He posed her in a three-quarter view that had her looking just over his right shoulder as he stood at the easel, hoping to capture a pensive expression. Then he started to sketch.

They knew a bit of each other's language. Panchito was always there to fill in when understanding faltered. He told Mitch, "La Señora is looking forward to seeing your work. Fidel said it was incredible and very truthful."

"I will try to live up to expectations," said Mitch, carefully drawing La Señora's image on the four-foot high by three-foot wide canvas.

While Mitch was sketching and La Señora was trying to hold still, they didn't talk much—although she did ask him how he traveled to Mexico. He replied that he came by private boat to the coast. Was driven to the hacienda by car.

"Beautiful country, Señora, up here in the central plateau. I'm looking forward to painting it when I get time," said Mitch without stopping his deft strokes on the canvas.

"You will find it has many aspects, Señor Mitch. It can be eternal in its distant horizons and clear blue skies. It can be soft and loving with its warm breezes, or it can be dangerous and tortured by a powerful sun. You will learn when these conditions come and go. As an artist you will make best use of those favorable to you."

Mitch liked her lyrical description and said, "Ever more reason for me to spend time painting it."

La Señora smiled without answering and held the pose. Mitch continued, "When I paint inspiring scenes, I feel nature's breath on my soul."

"I know that feeling, Señor Mitch. That is why I spend as much time here at the hacienda as possible," replied La Señora

After an hour and a half with a couple of breaks, Mitch took a long look at the charcoal sketch developing on the canvas. He declared it was enough for one day and asked when she could come back.

La Señora said she would be back the next day—thereafter four days a week.

"How long will the portrait take?" she asked.

"Two months, maybe longer."

"I think you better finish in two months, because that's as much posing as I want to do."

He felt firmness in her soft voice.

Mitch said, "We'll get it done by then."

After La Señora left with Panchito, Mitch sat out on the patio. Leaning back in the chair with his head cupped in his hands, he looked at the towering cumulous clouds above the walls. *I got good vibes from La Señora. That's good. We're going to be friends. Still, I've got to escape in the next two months—or think of some way to extend my stay. Can't chance good luck just happening—and doing nothing on my own. Gotta find a way.*

Chapter 14

FBI

Two weeks after Mitch Alexander's disappearance, Chad and Surfer were summoned to the FBI office in LA. Agents questioned them about Mitch's activities in the months prior. Chad explained how Mitch came to Malibu for art therapy four months ago. At first he came by bus, but after buying a car, he became a regular, painting there several days a week. For two weeks before his disappearance, he painted the Hideaway Cove at El Pescador, producing one picture of it every day.

Chad and Surfer were shown the picture gallery of iPhone photos they had taken since Mitch arrived on the scene. FBI agents had printed them out and put them on a long wall in chronological order. They were methodically putting Post-its on them, identifying every person.

"Who is this man?" asked agent Myron Wolf, pointing to the photo of a man seated on a picnic table being painted by Mitch.

Chad said, "That guy showed up one day while Mitch was painting by himself. He asked Mitch to paint his portrait. Mitch told him it would cost two hundred dollars. He told us about it during lunch at Malibu Seafood—said he could paint him in an hour."

Surfer jumped in. "I bet Mitch a lunch that he couldn't paint the guy in an hour. Chad and I drove to El Pescador to watch and see if he could."

"That's the man being painted?" Agent Wolf pointed again to the wall photo.

"That's him," Chad said. "As we walked up, I snapped that picture over Mitch's shoulder so I could catch both his painting and stranger. Took another one of Mitch's finished painting." Chad looked at the wall and pointed. "There it is, right there."

"Describe the stranger. Tell us all your impressions of him."

Chad and Surfer racked their memories as best they could: Latino with accent, not sure if Mexican or farther south. Everything about him expensive: designer jeans, boots of gray lizard skin, big watch that could have been a Rolex, fitted shirt with two buttons opened, gold chain, diamond earring left ear, and black cowboy hat. He stood about five foot ten and was broad shouldered, maybe two hundred pounds. He looked fit with a slight paunch and had a mustache. He had a little tattoo of a skull on the index knuckle of his right hand. Looked to be about forty years old. He had paid for the painting from a wad of hundreds and didn't shake hands or give his name. Took his wet painting and drove off.

After three hours the FBI ran out of questions and things to discuss. Agent Wolf said, "OK, guys, thanks for coming in. Took a lot of your time, and it wasn't always fun—but it might help us find out what happened to your friend."

———

A week later FBI agents were sitting around a conference table reviewing the case. Agent Wolf said, "We got nothing on this artist dropping outta sight."

"Easy, Myron. Let's run an ID check on Mitch Alexander's portrait subject," said John Hattersley, FBI chief of Los Angeles operations. "Run both the over-the-shoulder and the final painting photos against mug shots of Mexican heavy hitters—also Central and South Americans. He's dripping money and has a drug-gang tattoo. He's probably mobbed up with narco traffickers."

"We need to bring the Drug Enforcement Agency into this one. Looks like an international case," said Agent Tim Wills.

"Right, Tim," said the chief. "Myron, call DEA. See if they can help us identify this guy."

"Roger, Chief."

The DEA wrestled with the ID challenge for ten days. Finally they positively identified the stranger in the photo as Fidel Terrasombra, brother of El Jefe, Mexico's most notorious drug lord. He was not in the United States legally. It was more than a disappearing-person case, now that a foreign criminal might be involved. The FBI team knew then they had to contact the Department of Homeland Security.

Chief Hattersley said, "Myron, call Jane Heartworthy at DHS and tell her we have a job for her."

Chapter 15

THE FIESTA

After two weeks of work, the portrait's direction was revealing itself. Mitch had blocked in the entire canvas with shapes of exaggerated color. He worked as slowly as possible so that it would just finish in two months. The face was shaping up, with Mitch taking advantage of the slow pace to ensure drawing accuracy for an exact likeness.

La Señora's *café-au-lait* complexion was becoming apparent. Mitch gladly changed her dress color several times to suit her wishes. She realized that when portrayed on canvas with her jewelry against a background of cool, dark gray dress colors looked different from what she had imagined beforehand. After each posing session, he scraped off excess paint, saving the tooth of the canvas for another day.

La Señora discussed with Mitch which jewelry, clothes, and accessories worked best—with help from Panchito's translations. They became friends, and each looked forward to seeing the other at the painting sessions.

Panchito told Mitch there would be a big party that night. Told him to remain at his adobe. "Don't worry, Mitch. I will bring you food and wine from the banquet. You and me will have dinner together."

"*Esta bien*, Panchito."

Limos from Mexico City arrived at twilight. Candles and lanterns were lit. Mariachis sang. The party got underway with high fashion ladies and elegant men gathering for aperitifs. Dinner for forty was served an hour later, and the buzz of happy people drifted to his studio.

Panchito brought a splendid dinner. They ate together to celebrate El Jefe's fiftieth birthday from their corner of the hacienda. After finishing, Panchito left with the dinner tray, leaving Mitch to sit alone, nursing a beer and looking at the stars.

He came out of his reverie when he saw Panchito approaching accompanied by a knockout lady.

"Mitch, meet a niece of El Jefe, Señorita Amparo Terrasombra."

They shook hands and smiled.

Mitch thought, *She is so beautiful—great figure too. Too rich for my lifestyle.*

Amparo thought, *He's not as Bohemian looking as I expected. Uncle Max told me the artist was very odd, but it doesn't look like he is starving or suffering for his art. Looks like your basic gringo, with brown eyes instead of blue. Reminds me of Harrison Ford, the actor.*

Amparo asked Mitch, "May I see La Señora's painting, or is it too soon?"

"Of course, Señorita. I would like to know what you think about it." He opened the door with a gallant gesture and said, "Pase." She entered while his appreciative eyes checked out a black gown tight around her hips and thighs and flared below the knees. Great ass!

As Amparo looked at the embryonic work, Mitch said, "I'm working in the method of Whistler: scraping down fresh paint in early phases until major adjustments of form, color, and value are settled upon." Mitch wasn't sure she knew who Whistler was.

Amparo nodded approvingly and looked around the studio—eventually seeing Dream Wrecks stacked on end, leaning against the walls. She flipped through them quickly. "These are really good, Mitch—can I call you that?"

"Sure, Señorita Amparo."

"Amparo is enough."

She's businesslike. Right to the point, he thought.

Amparo flipped through the Dream Wrecks again, but more slowly, taking some out for a more careful look. She finally said, "These paintings portray a struggle. Good and evil or victory and defeat. Some kind of conflict seeking a solution."

Mitch said, "They do have a struggle; you got that right."

Still flipping through the canvases, Mitch noted her face in profile. Her nose was slightly convex, and her facial distances from hairline to eyebrows, eyebrows to bottom of nose, and bottom of nose to chin were perfectly equal. Classic!

"They are better than a lot of shallow works I see so often," said Amparo, turning toward him, revealing large dark eyes, wide cheekbones, and full, lush lips.

"Thanks, Amparo," he said distractedly, now noting the entrancing linearity of her cheeks.

"Why do you paint them?" she asked, pulling him back from his analysis of her beauty to the grimmer direction of where her question was leading.

"I paint them to stay attached to my soul." He looked down. "Or what's left of it."

Taken back Amparo frowned and said, "Tell me more."

Might as well blab it out, Mitch thought. Panchito had heard it all before, so there was no added embarrassment with him standing there. "I came out of Afghanistan pretty screwed up mentally. Got a lot of nightmares, depression."

"And painting helped?" Amparo asked, intently looking into his eyes.

"I found out that jumping out of bed and painting a Dream Wreck…"

"Que?" she interrupted with a little frown appearing on her silken forehead. "Dream Wreck?"

"Yeah, that's what I call 'em. Anyway I whip out a Dream Wreck and…"

"And then OK?" she interrupted again.

"Yeah I'm OK until the next night."

"Mitch, these Dream Wrecks, as you call them, have a uniqueness. I am sure they would sell in my gallery. Can I take some back to Mexico City tomorrow?"

"Sure, take them all. I need the money," he said, hoping she might have better luck than he had trying to sell them at the Brewery.

"By the way, Mitch, Whistler had no time for critics. Are you that way too?" she asked with a twinkle in her eye, catching him off-balance.

"Uh…I try to stay open to feedback," was all he could come up with.

———

The next morning Amparo backed her black Range Rover close to the studio door. *Not too shabby,* thought Mitch, watching from the window. He saw Panchito had the table set for two. They loaded a dozen Dream Wrecks into the Range Rover and then sat down for breakfast. Panchito wandered off to a shaded chair to read the *El Universal* newspaper, out of earshot.

Amparo said, "Mitch, there are a few details I have to discuss with you."

"OK, let's talk."

"My uncle, Tio Max, insists your identity be a secret."

Mitch thought, *Of course he does; he just kidnapped me.*

Amparo continued, "We'll sign your works 'Ricardo Casa DeSpiritu' and tell the world you are a total recluse—at least until it is time to reveal your true identify."

"Cool name, sounds important," he said, while thinking, *Damn, she sure is one take-charge lady.*

Amparo added, "Tio Max is extremely secretive. Please try to understand and don't let it bother you. He keeps his business and his family matters to himself. He is fanatic that way. You are a guest at his hacienda and are painting La Señora, so he considers your presence here a family matter. After you leave it's another situation. Then we'll let everyone know who Ricardo Casa DeSpiritu really is."

Mitch thought, *She really believes I am a* guest *here!*

He said, "I understand; it's OK. How did you pick the name Ricardo Casa DeSpiritu?"

"Oh, I wanted a name people would remember. Enough syllables to be rhythmic, romantic sounding, its meaning a little mysterious, and with a unique spelling."

"You are thinking all the time, Amparo," said Mitch.

"I can't help it," said Amparo. "Always thinking about business. And one more thing: When we are finished with breakfast and I am talking to Panchito, I want you to put your fingerprint in paint on the edge of each canvas as your proof for the future. I will print Ricardo Casa DeSpiritu on the back of each work. We go fifty-fifty on sales."

"OK," said Mitch.

"Also, and I hope you don't take this too hard, but I can't call your works Dream Wrecks. I am sure there are people in LA that know you call them that."

"Crap," said Mitch, irritated. "I've paid my dues to call them that."

"How about if we call your works Fevered Thoughts or *Pensamientos Febriles*," she offered.

"Hmm… Sounds weird to me," said Mitch.

"Mitch, it will sound very dramatic to a Spanish speaker's ears."

"I guess this English speaker will learn to like it."

"For us to work together, you must be satisfied." She looked at him to see his reaction.

Her beautiful face enlivened with a question on it couldn't be denied. Mitch caved, "OK, will do—this time."

Amparo walked over to Panchito and asked if Mitch had everything he needed for painting. Assured he did, she returned and slipped Mitch a stack of bills. "Here is twenty thousand pesos in advance."

"Lady, you are all business. Many thanks, but I'm still not too crazy about Pensa…"

"Pen-sa-mi-en-tos Fe-bril-es," she enunciated cheerfully.

"But I like your style," he said, grinning. And without thinking he added, "And I like your smile."

She chuckled, blushed, and shook hands. She saw the black smudge from his thumb on her wrist, impulsively pecked him on the cheek, and said, "We are going to do good business together."

As she turned to climb into her car, Mitch said, "See you soon, Amparo."

"Adios, Mitch." And she drove off.

Chapter 16

WORK IN PROGRESS

Amparo came back for more paintings two weeks later. Mitch was painting La Señora when she pulled up at his door. She entered quietly, sat down, and watched. He occasionally glanced in her direction when stepping back away from the canvas for a longer view—with brief eye contact, maybe a hint of a smile. After the session they sat at the patio table. Over coffee that Panchito had ready, Amparo said, "Mitch, I never tire of watching you painting. I could watch for hours."

"Not much company when I'm painting, I'm afraid."

"Por qué?"

"I go in the zone and don't communicate."

"That's what I like about watching you—your silence with full concentration. Your face reflects a complete involvement. It's showing contentment in your work."

La Señora chimed in, "I too am fascinated by you holding those long brushes at the end, yet making accurate, beautiful strokes. I see you sometimes looking at me while your brush moves across the canvas."

"Muy amable, Señoras," said Mitch with a theatrical bow.

The ladies laughed.

La Señora said, "No joking, you have God's gift to create something."

Amparo added, "Your stroke-by-stroke creation on canvas mesmerizes me."

"Señoras, it's flattering to hear that you are entertained by a skinny Gringo—while I have the company of two beautiful ladies and the sunshine of their smiles."

Amparo laughed full-on out loud, "Mitch, you are *sin vergüenza*—without shame—and a bullsheeter too." All laughed loudly.

La Señora asked, "Qué es 'bullsheeter?'" Even louder guffaws erupted from Mitch and Amparo.

Amparo told La Señora a Spanish equivalent.

"*Dios mio,* Ampi, I don't think he is bullsheeter."

More chuckles and chatting until Amparo announced, "It is time for me to go. I have to get back before dark, and I have to make my recluse artist famous."

Mitch and Amparo loaded Dream Wrecks into her car. She closed the back door and, out of Panchito's view behind the car, playfully gave Mitch a prolonged, full-contact hug. Mitch heard her aside to La Señora, "Watch out, *Abuelita*; he is a charmer." He felt a tingle down his spine.

She drove off, and Panchito escorted La Señora to the main house.

———

Amparo returned two weeks later. Again she watched Mitch paint, fascinated by his depth of concentration. She noticed a rhythm in his work. He studied model and canvas, mixed paint rapidly, stroked it on, and then walked back several steps to check progress. Occasionally their eyes met in this ritual, and smiles toyed with their lips.

Over coffee afterward, Amparo excitedly told him and La Señora, "The exhibition of Mitch's work will be the most elaborate show I've ever had."

"Does a recluse artist deserve it?" asked Mitch playfully.

Putting her hand on his shoulder, she said, "Only if he is a skinny gringo."

La Señora asked, "How will this opening be different, Ampi?"

"I've got five top designers—each has been given nine Ricardo Casa DeSpiritu works to frame and hang. Each has complete freedom to paint and carpet their section of my gallery to exhibit their assigned works to their best effect.

"Our National Opera's principal choreographer will orchestrate the opening's progression through the five sections. He will use mimes and harlequins to focus the crowd as the curator interprets the works. Mexico's top event director, Macias del Toro y Esperanza, will make it all happen including music, lighting, and gourmet food catering."

"Amparo, what the hell are you smoking?" exclaimed Mitch.

"Listen, Gringo; when your Queen Beaner gets a bug up her ass, watch out."

He choked, sprayed a mouthful of coffee, and went into coughing fit. Standing up, he blew his nose. Finally when he stopped coughing Amparo said, "Mitch, I am a bulldog. When my mind is set on something, I give it everything."

La Señora asked, "Que es 'bug up her ass?'"

Chapter 17

NOT FORGOTTEN

The story of Mitch Alexander's disappearance resonated with the public for a variety of reasons. Some people just wanted to see the spot at El Pescador State Beach where the artist was last seen. They were curious about seeing a place from which a human being vanished. They often left flowers or notes at the cliff top.

Newspapers have a problem writing about disappeared persons that haven't left clues to the reason they disappeared: there is not much to write about. They need an angle to give their readers something to sink their teeth into. The *LA Times* did an in-depth series of articles on art therapy. Unknown to the public, and of great interest to many, was how widespread art therapy was in its many forms.

Chad was featured as an authority on Plein Air Expression in the *LA Times series*. He also appeared on Oprah's channel. several of his clients gave testimonials to Plein Air Expression's uplifting effect. Chad's clientele increased with this exposure. He had to hold sessions twice a week and hire a full-time helper.

Burl O'Grady featured the story on Pinnacle News. He said that everyone feels good after a day at the beach. So why was that so special? O'Grady pooh-poohed Plein Air Expression as an example of moral fiber rotting in California. He said people should not be chasing new fads as ways to avoid confronting life's problems realistically.

A week later, Pinnacle News reported there were rumors that Mitch Alexander had committed suicide. O'Grady promised a bombshell revelation that Plein Air Expression was the cause of Alexander's mental deterioration. In subsequent weeks O'Grady blamed the lack of additional information on a cover-up by the government.

A month after the disappearance Allied Artists of Malibu held a paint out for a hundred artists at El Pescador. A live model, of Mitch's size and build, posed to represent Mitch painting at the place where he disappeared. Each of the Allied Artists captured Mitch in his or her own style. They were mourning one of their own.

An anonymous benefactor commissioned sculptor Friedel Champlain to portray the artist at work. Champlain immediately began work on a life-size statue to be cast in bronze. It would commemorate a hero who fought for his country and was fighting his way back to normalcy when the Lord took him.

The Mitch Alexander story had aroused the interest of the curious, the skeptical, and the sincere—and there was no sign of it subsiding in the foreseeable future.

Chapter 18

LA SEÑORA'S PORTRAIT FINISHED

The day before the painting was to be finished and signed, La Señora came to the studio. Panchito stayed out on the patio to smoke and read the paper. She greeted Mitch with a hug plus a big smile. "I am so happy with your work. It is about finished. What can I ever do to thank you?"

"Señora, I have an idea."

"Please tell me, Mitch."

"I would like to do a family portrait of you, your sons Maximilliano and Fidel, and your granddaughter Amparo. All of you have in some way made my life here what it is today and have shown me a beautiful part of this magnificent country. In this way I can extend my thanks to your whole family."

"But that is not me doing something for you."

"That is true, Señora, what I need from you is to tell Maximilliano that you would like the family portrait to be done and for me to stay here for another two months."

"I understand, Mitch. I will do it for you."

The next morning El Jefe came to Mitch's adobe with La Señora and Panchito. Hector followed with an implanted scowl. They gathered in the studio and stood in front of the completed portrait as Mitch signed "Ricardo Casa DeSpiritu" in the lower right corner.

The painting was sublime: soft, ineffably colored skin; hint of a smile; artifacts of age modeled to reflect a kind heart and a clear, determined mind; soft folds of clothing capturing attention, but not competing with the face; adorning jewelry accenting and completing the radiance of La Señora's image.

They stood there silently looking at the painting. "So beautiful, mi Madre, it takes my breath away," said El Jefe.

"Sí, Maxcito, it is *fantastico*. I want you to hang it in the hacienda—and I want to ask a favor of you."

"Yes, Mamá."

"I want another painting. This time of our family."

"But Mamá, Raul and Hector are taking our artista to the airport tomorrow," said El Jefe with a hint of exasperation.

"Could you stay another two months, Mitch, to paint me surrounded by Maxi, Fidelito, Ampi, and my dog, Bandito?"

"Of course, Señora, I can fit two months into my schedule," Mitch replied enthusiastically.

"Mamá, you shall have your desire," El Jefe said flatly, hiding his displeasure. "But I can't sit for a painting with my traveling schedule."

"Not to worry, Señor. I can work from a photo," piped up Mitch. "I'll need Amparo to sit several times, but Fidel, of course, doesn't have to sit either. I've painted him already. Never forget a face I paint."

———

The next day Amparo arrived in her dusty Range Rover, a hug with firm squeezes by both of them. "Oh, Mitch, great news! Ricardo Casa DeSpiritu sold out his first exhibition. The mystery artist is a sensation all over the art world. Your Pensamientos Febriles are famous."

"God that's incredible news, Amparo. I used to sell an occasional Dream Wreck for two hundred dollars—you sell forty-five of them for ten thousand dollars each. Am I getting rich?"

"Yes—we are," she said with a smile and a deep look into his eyes. "Here are a few more bucks, as gringos say." She slipped him a packet of bills with an Aztec money clip. "When you come to Mexico City, I'll give you your bank account book—there's more there for you."

"Wow! I don't think I can handle any more good news."

"Two months from now, you have another exhibition in Berlin. I need everything you have now—and everything you can paint in a month."

"You shall have it. But now come in and see La Señora's finished painting."

Startled, Amparo exclaimed, "Finished—that means you're leaving!" Then she entered his studio and gasped with the sight of La Señora on canvas. "Incredible, Mitch—you have a gift. You can't leave Mexico now."

"Got good news for you," said Mitch in a playful mood. "I'm not going to leave Mexico—until I do a family portrait for La Señora. Yesterday she decided she needed one, and I'm the man to do it."

"Are you serious?" she said, brightening up.

"Sí, you are in it also, with La Señora and the boys. It is going to be a large work. I need you to pose a few times."

"Gladly, Mitch. I've dreamed of posing for you—now it's come true."

Then Panchito, who had been sitting in his chair reading the paper, noticed them sitting down at the patio table and called out, "Lunch in five minutes." He headed for the kitchen door of the main house.

After lunch, Panchito helped load the Dream Wrecks into Amparo's Range Rover. Hector, who has been sulking about after being denied his chance to drive Mitch to the airport, watched from the main house terrace. Amparo ate quickly and said, "I have a hundred things to do in the city." She gave him a quick hug and drove off.

———

Mitch sat in front of his adobe to ponder the lowering sun and its crimson path reflected from cloud bottoms reaching to the horizon. He thought, *On the hacienda's low ground, where I can see over the walls, there are great distances and a feeling of boundless freedom. But, in most directions I can just see sky over the walls. No matter how well they treat me, it is still a prison.*

He felt down. There were guards at the gates and some-times along the outer walls. Hector, bad cop, and Panchito, good cop, always there. No phones, no Internet, and knowing that Hector and Raul would drive him to…the "airport."

Amparo giving me a quick good-bye didn't help either, Mitch thought. *Don't give up on me, baby. If you hugged me for two seconds longer, I'd be feeling better now. She did an immense amount of work on the exhibition—maybe I should have expressed more appreciation. It will be a tough week until she comes back.*

A cloud of depression wafted over his spirit. As he sat there in the twilight his thoughts churned, *I gotta find a way to escape from this place. Can't give in to the blues and do nothing. I've got the money from painting sales, but how can it help? Could Amparo help me? I know she likes me as a friend—maybe a little bit more—but enough to go against El Jefe and her family? What does she know about what I am doing there? I was lucky today and got a two-month reprieve. When the family portrait is done I'm busting out of this friggin' prison—don't know how, but I'm bustin' out. Maybe before the portrait is done. I won't be here for the next ride to the airport!*

Chapter 19

ON TO THE FAMILY PORTRAIT

Panchito and Hector drove Mitch to San Miguel to stock up on supplies. Mitch bought canvases for Dream Wrecks and a ton of oil paints and ordered a four-by-six-foot canvas for the family portrait. He threw in sketchpads and watercolor paints for those intervals when time would hang heavy on his hands. Panchito put it all on El Jefe's credit card.

After a few beers at Tio Lucas Restaurant, Panchito said, "This part of Mexico is revered for its fight for freedom from Spain."

Mitch mused, *How about my freedom, Panchito?*

Hector didn't say much. Just sat there with an impassive face ready to growl. *And ready to chase me down if I run for it,* thought Mitch.

Panchito continued with the story. "Allende is a great hero here. You have seen his statue in the Jardín. Died fighting for Mexico. During the month of September, we have patriotic fiestas here and in cities nearby like Guanajuato and Dolores Hidalgo."

Over lunch, featuring *chiles en nogada* to celebrate the red, white, and green of the Mexican flag, Panchito's monologue about the history of the region continued. Mitch enjoyed it, as Panchito told the story well. And then it was time to return to the hacienda.

Feeling the beer and tequila, Mitch devoted all his attention to navigating narrow sidewalks and getting by oncoming pedestrians—while cars were passing inches away. He spotted a bookstore as they headed toward the car.

"Panchito, can you buy me a few books?" asked Mitch, not wanting to reveal the cash Amparo had given him. "I've read all the English ones in the studio."

"OK, Mitch, pick out some books, and I'll charge them to El Jefe," he said with a wink.

On the way back, Mitch fell asleep and dreamed he was in a giant cathedral-like building. Shafts of hazy sunlight from high windows revealed others, dressed in white robes, walking about with meditative expressions on their faces. Not happy, not sad, they strolled their paths waiting for the future to be upon them.

———

On her first visit for the family portrait a few days later, Amparo brought albums of photos that she, Mitch, and La

Señora went through. They found a handful for use as reference images for the brothers who wouldn't be posing.

Amparo looked gorgeous in white slacks, cork heels, and a plunging peasant-girl blouse, whose revelations Mitch fought gamely to keep his eyes off, as she leaned in to look at the albums.

They had lunch together as usual at the patio table. La Señora and Amparo carried the conversational ball with small talk about their family that was spread around the center and west coast of Mexico.

Mitch had to know more about Amparo. "Sounds like you are a strong personality like others in your family."

"I like the challenge of working hard toward a goal."

"A competition thing?" asked Mitch, trying to find out more about what made this dynamic lady tick.

"Not really," said Amparo, "because my goal is not to take business away from other galleries or brokers."

"Isn't it better for you to sell artwork instead of someone else?" asked Mitch.

Amparo responded without missing a beat, "I like to find emerging artists that don't belong to other galleries and show their magic to the world for the first time."

La Señora said, "You have made good business that way, but you work too hard."

Turning to her grandmother, she said, "I am obsessive, Abuela."

La Señora responded, "You have so much energy to give…"

"And I burn it up working."

"Working is not everything, Ampi," said La Señora.

"So true, Abuela. I also seek fulfillment."

"Have you found it?" asked La Señora.

"My journey has just begun…" Amparo looked up and held her hand out. "And it feels like the rain has too."

The threatening thunderclouds held off no longer. Big drops were hitting the last Dream Wrecks as they loaded them in Amparo's Range Rover. A full-length hug from Amparo told Mitch he was going to have a good week ahead.

"*Hasta la próxima semana,* skinny Gringo. See you next week."

She drove through the gate accompanied by a flash of lightning and an immediate thunderclap. A week of steady rain began.

A large canvas was delivered a few days later, and Mitch began by toning it with swirls of reddish-brown wash. He busied himself with a number of pencil sketches of the Terrasombras—searching for the right composition. After a few days, he began to sketch in the figures on the big canvas with vine charcoal. He wanted to have the figures completely sketched in when Amparo would come back next weekend. He kept busy all week in sync with the tempo of the drumming rain—and with his mind relishing flashbacks to that last, luxurious *abrazo.*

Funny how abrazos progressed, he thought. The first was just cheek touching and a halfway hug with his arms. Then the tops of their chests touched, and the arms went all the way around for a full hug. Further abrazos had positive contact with her breasts and his chest. Now when Hector and Panchito are not watching they sneak a full-length abrazo that could last two or three seconds.

————

Next week Amparo arrived to find Mitch finishing an elaborate sketch of the family group on the four-foot-by-six-foot canvas. The figures were arranged with La Señora seated, looking straight ahead with an open, serene expression. Fidel and Maximilliano stood on each side dressed in dark suits—Maximilliano closer with a hand on the high back of La Señora's chair and Fidel with his head turned slightly toward her with one hand in his pocket. Amparo stood a little beyond Fidel—looking at La Señora while holding her right hand at shoulder height with a little bird perched on her forefinger.

"I like that unconventional composition, Mitch," said Amparo, standing before the painting with one hand on her hip. What do you think, Abuela?"

"It will be a painting that makes people think," said La Señora. "That I like."

At lunch Mitch asked Amparo, "Can you come here to pose one day a week for four weeks?"

"Of course, Mitch. What should I wear?"

"Something light. We'll have men in dark suits and ladies in light outfits. You and La Señora can work out the details."

Amparo took off after lunch, as usual, with the latest Dream Wrecks.

Mitch thought back to the last hug. Was it longer than the one before? Did she push her lower body against him? Maybe just a little, or was it his imagination? Did her arms squeeze him a little tighter this time?

Amparo was rarely alone with him in the studio. Either La Señora or Panchito was usually there. He'd been warned to keep his distance—he did, and it was driving him crazy.

Someday when he got out of the hacienda, he would see her and get to know her in a deep and meaningful way. He thought, *I'm sure she likes me—could be a delusion—won't be the first time. But I am going to run with this delusion—or whatever it is—as far as I can.*

In the days following, Mitch exercised every day. The thought was often in his mind that he would have to find a way to escape over the wall and cross-country. Climbing a wall, not easy, and then miles of hiking. *I'll be in shape for it*, he thought. Even got Panchito to walk with him around his adobe a few mornings a week—he didn't want to be too obvious.

———

The next week Mitch was at work with Amparo, holding her standing pose, with La Señora quietly sitting and watching.

"Amazing man you are."

"Oh come on, Amparo."

"This is my third session, and progress has been rapid. Tio Max and Fidel are almost complete, and everyone looks so natural but, at the same, time special."

"But I still have another three weeks to finish it," said Mitch.

"I know you can paint much faster. Why do you take such a long time?"

"The more I return to the same subjects, the more I find out about them—that reflects in the finished paintings."

"About me too?" She teased. "What have you discovered?"

"Well, lemme see. The colors of shadows on your skin, smile shapes on your face—stuff like that. Even the smell of your perfume."

La Señora cracked up laughing. "Mitchito, how do you paint the smell of perfume?"

"That is a professional secret," Mitch replied.

La Señora laughingly said, "No es secreto, Mitchito; you are bullsheeter!"

They all burst out laughing.

After lunch, while Amparo was picking up Dream Wrecks to load in her car, she asked, "Why are some painted lighter, more diffused?"

"Had this dream last time we went to San Miguel for supplies. Drank too much with Panchito, fell asleep on the ride back, and dreamed I was in another place."

"Tell me about it."

"OK," said Mitch, after stacking the last Dream Wreck in the car. "Imagine a giant cathedral or Aztec temple. There is light filtering through high windows in shafts down on the marble floor. People are wandering around in white robes silently in and out of light shafts and surrounding dusk. As I wandered, I would look in the eyes of others for a few seconds and then move on. There was no danger or fear like my usual nightmares. It wasn't happy either. An in-between state of waiting for a future."

"*Muy profundo,* Mitch," she said, looking at him searchingly for a few seconds—and then with a hint of a smile. "I'll be thinking about that all the way back to Mexico City. People wandering around waiting for a connection of some kind. Almost like Kafka's characters—trying to connect with each other or with God."

Then came the abrazo Mitch was waiting for. He gave her a good squeeze with his right hand a little farther down her back than usual.

Her Range Rover disappeared out the gate.

"Hey, Panchito. After you walk La Señora back to the house, let's have a couple of beers and walk around."

"OK, Mitch."

————

The next week followed the usual tempo: Amparo posing, La Señora sitting and watching. Mitch worked slowly on Amparo's clothing folds, which he painted simply in two shades, light and shadow. He worked his magic by slipping in subtle color variations, mainly in the shadows.

La Señora started sneezing and stepped out for a minute.

Amparo asked, "Did you paint a lot of naked women in art school?"

"Sure, that's how I learned the body's shape. I have to visualize what's underneath the clothes for them to drape right in the painting."

Mitch saw her make the slightest movement when he said that. Amparo, in her pose with the right hand held up for the imaginary bird, felt a flush and hoped Mitch did not see her blushing. La Señora came back in, sneezed again—in time to restore a lighthearted mood.

"OK ladies, now for the fun part. I am going to paint Bandito."

Amparo pulled up a chair next to La Señora, and Mitch rapidly outlined the little dog lying at La Señora's feet. He painted a whitish form freely without going back over anything. Then with darker colors, he cut in shadows on the floor and suggestions of a nose, mouth, eyes, and the dog's jeweled collar. Rapid accents hit the collar jewels and tiny highlights in the eyes.

The two ladies were mesmerized into silent, open-mouth stares and, half an hour later, jolted back into reality when Mitch dropped the brush, bowed with a flourish, and said, "Let's have lunch."

Chapter 20

HOMELAND SECURITY

Commander Jane Heartworthy was a rising star in Homeland Security. She was the youngest female commander in coast guard history and an avid triathlon competitor. She earned top honors at the Coast Guard Academy and US Naval War College and distinguished herself in debating at both places. As intense at play as at work—where grueling, twelve-hour days were her norm—days off often found her playing two eighteen-hole rounds of golf and holding forth in the club-house bar until closing.

She liked to throw impromptu parties to break up the routine of tough projects. Felt it was good for morale. These get-togethers were open to all ranks. She often came close to the line of fraternization with lower ranks, without stepping over—or at least not too far over. Commander Heartworthy was a natural team builder. Her ability to work with different government organizations and inspire people at all levels got her the assignment she was about to lead.

———

"Good morning, Jane," said Chief FBI Agent John Hattersley, as Commander Heartworthy entered his conference room at the LA FBI headquarters. He turned to a dozen men and women at the conference table. "This case will be handled under Commander Jane Heartworthy's leadership from now on.

"So far this case has involved the police, DEA, NSA, navy, coast guard, and us in the FBI. The CIA will likely be involved in the near future. This case has morphed into a classic joint operation. Commander Heartworthy represents Homeland Security. She is experienced in leading complex joint operations like this one. Please give her your full support."

All eyes turned toward the commander. Her smart, blue uniform looked like it was designed for her athletic frame. She had military school bearing, tanned face, and close-cropped blond hair. Exuding confidence she was attractive but not at all in a soft or vulnerable way.

"Thank you, Myron. I asked for this informal meeting to one, thank you for taking this strange case as far as you have; two, brief you on our current situation and plans; and three, get a chance to meet all of you one-on-one.

"To begin, Myron Wolf of the FBI will brief us on new information that has developed. We'll then review our next steps for getting on top of this situation."

Myron spoke in a businesslike tone. "Everyone here is familiar with this case, so I'll just cover the latest findings concerning Fidel Terrasombra, brother of the notorious El Jefe.

"We have found that Fidel has no criminal record in the United States and none in Mexico either.

"Mexican Federal Police provided information on Fidel: He is forty years old. Born and raised in Morelia in the state of Michoacán—now controlled by organized drug criminals. No record of a marriage. Spent two years in the Mexican Army as a lieutenant. Speaks English. Filed no tax returns and there are no records of him in any business enterprise. No trace of him in official records after his army service ended twenty years ago.

"Immediately after DEA identification of Fidel as the man artist Mitch Alexander painted the day before he disappeared, we arranged for continuous surveillance of the so-called Hideaway Cove house.

"The National Security Agency (NSA) searched for all telephone calls and e-mails coming from the Hideaway Cove house—from the date of disappearance on. NSA analysts eventually found an e-mail from the Hideaway Cove house. Attached was a photo of Mitch Alexander's one-hour portrait of Fidel. It was sent the same day Mitch painted Fidel's portrait to an untraceable Mexican e-mail address. We do know that e-mail was opened and printed in an Internet café in Guanajuato, Mexico."

———

"I'll take it from here Myron, thank you." Commander Heartworthy said. "Let's review what we know: Mitch

Alexander disappeared after painting Fidel Terrasombra, brother of El Jefe. Same day an e-mail of the painting is downloaded in Guanajuato—not far from where we believe El Jefe lives. That's it. Not a lot of information but there are big implications."

"So what do we do next?" asked an agent.

"A night-and-day stakeout has been set up at El Pescador State Beach. Human eyes will be on the Hideaway Cove house twenty-four seven. These eyes belong to surfers, tourists, and other innocuous-looking operatives. In addition, electronic surveillance and satellite imaging will cover every avenue in and out of that house.

"Any questions?"

Dudley Henshaw, DEA supervisor and highest-ranking civilian on the team, asked in a thick southern drawl, "Anyone residin' in the Hideaway Cove house?"

Commander Heartworthy replied, "Yes, our police and FBI partners report that there are Latino men living there most of the time. By the way, we will not arrest anyone now, not even Fidel T—we're shooting for the big fish, El Jefe. Right now we are watching and learning."

With no further questions, the commander said, "OK, that's it for the first go. Let's do some team building at El Torito on the first floor. Lunch and margaritas on me."

Chapter 21

SUB CHASE

At Los Angeles Air Force Base, Commander Heartworthy's team members were at their Joint Operation Center (JOC) stations. Tactical information from a variety of sources and sensors flowed to big screens on the front wall and to individual screens for team members seated at curved tables facing the stage.

Commander Heartworthy strode to the front of the JOC. At the podium she paused for a moment to silence the room. "Good morning, I am Commander Jane Heartworthy. Before I begin, I want to thank the US Air Force for providing this leading edge facility."

From an array of podium switches, she activated a large screen behind her. "Last night there was a breakthrough development in our search for the Terrasombra Cartel connection.

"I'll bring you up to speed on our surveillance and then tell you the big news," the commander said, turning toward the screens. "Now take a look at the screen showing our NSA intercept area—on the Malibu coast. The blinking red point is where we intercepted the e-mail containing the painted image of Fidel Terrasombra. It came from a white house at El Pescador State Beach."

Photos of the Hideaway Cove house popped up on another screen. Commander Heartworthy clicked a button and a yellow circle of half-mile radius appeared. She said, "This circle around the house indicates our twenty-four seven surveillance coverage. We have human assets there equipped with sensors including infrared goggles and telescopes.

"Now we're getting to the good part: Today at 2:03 a.m., a Jet Ski with two men aboard left the beach behind the house and headed out to sea. We scrambled a Border Patrol P-3 aircraft from Pt. Mugu to follow it. We assumed the Jet Ski would rendezvous with another vessel and we wanted to see it.

"Take a look at the P-3 sensor images on your right-hand screen. That grainy plot depicts three vessels in a search box off El Pescador State Beach. A closer look now reveals that two are squid fishing boats—the third a submarine. Yes, believe it or not, it's a *submarine*!"

Excited voices exclaimed surprise, unbelief. A chorus of *wows, holy shits,* and *goddamns* erupted, followed with the buzz of loud conversations.

"Teammates. Teammates," the commander said loudly over the PA system. "Calm down. Our P-3 was on station in twenty minutes from call-up and witnessed the Jet Ski pulling up to the sub. Look hard at this little gray area amidships. You'll see that Jet Ski alongside the sub. The sub is twelve miles farther out to sea than the squid boats; it is not displaying running lights and was certainly not seen by them.

"Submarines of this type are manufactured in Germany and Norway for military to research—even tourist purposes. They are mission capable up to two thousand miles. Not sure whose sub it is, but we immediately tracked it: first by P-3 staying discreetly far enough away not to alert it, then handing off to a satellite system equipped with sub-detection capability.

"Right now we are tracking it heading south at periscope depth. We are preparing for continued surveillance landside when it reaches port.

"Our goal: find its final destination and identify the person they took on board—without them knowing they are being followed.

"When we pick up the trail at the sub's destination port, we expect to discover more about how El Jefe's cartel operates. And we expect to get more answers to the baffling question of where the artist Mitch Alexander ended up. If he was abducted by submarine, we might learn where he is now.

"As we speak, our CIA colleagues are drilling down into the Terrasombra family, digging up everything they can on their whereabouts and finances. Our ultimate goal is to crush that drug cartel."

———

Four days later Commander Heartworthy spoke from the same podium, "We have maintained satellite contact as the sub cruised south. You can see its track off Baja California on the center screen. We will have assets at the destination port when it arrives."

Dudley Henshaw asked, "What kind of assets are you talking about?"

"We have mobilized innocuous-looking CIA agents who are also heading south by car along Baja's coast. You can see them represented as blue dots on the coastal map shown above. When we discover the destination port, they will infiltrate the local scene and track people of interest disembarking from the sub. Now let's take a look at the next four slides and you'll see pictures of what our CIA assets look like:

"Slide one depicts the Taco Vendor. He is a Mexican man shown standing next to the taco cart he will be attending after he unloads it from his pickup truck. Taco carts are ubiquitous in Mexico, so his won't arouse suspicion near the submarine pier. He has limpet transponders in his cart that can be attached magnetically to a vehicle to track it by satellite.

"Slide two shows the middle-aged Tourist Couple in a convertible. They look like thousands of other American tourists in Mexico. They are seasoned CIA agents fluent in Spanish and they have in their car airborne robotic surveillance devices that we will show you in a minute.

"Slide three shows the French Scientist who will be driving a Citröen 2CV. He has the smarts to understand the submarine technology and he blends in nicely as a harmless eco tourist.

"Slide four shows the Surfers who could be part of the large American surfer community in Baja. They are five seasoned agents trained as navy seals and will provide the muscle and help in extracting from Mexico hostile or friendly persons—as needed. They will be traveling in a VW bus and towing a trailer with their surfboards in it.

"All of our CIA assets are equipped with personal video recording devices that can transmit images and voices back to this JOC for us to see in real time."

Dudley piped up again. "Jeeesus Christ, are these sorry-assed clowns the front line of our war on international cartels?"

The commander replied calmly, "Thank you for making that point. These agents are certainly not types to draw suspicion. You all have to agree about that."

Laughter burst from the crowded JOC.

"Continuing onward, our high-tech assets will also be in place. We'll launch a drone that can track a car from five thousand feet without being seen or heard." An image of a drone that looked like a model airplane popped up on another screen. "We have robots for close-in video and audio. These are illustrated on the next two slides. They are robots in the forms of a gold finch and a tarantula—both are sun powered with almost infinite ranges. "Bird Bot naturally flies to work while Spider Bot walks, slower but sometimes needed where Bird Bot can't infiltrate. Their transmissions are relayed by satellite to our team here in the JOC. Tourist Couple has these robots and the drone in their car trunk."

Chapter 22

BERLIN

A headline in the tabloid Bild Am Sonntag shouted: "Unbelievable Rise of Ricardo Casa DeSpiritu, the Mystery Artist." The synopsis read: "His fame was kicked off in Mexico City with the Pensamientos Febriles I exhibition at Galeria Amparo. Complete sellout at opening. Intense curiosity about—and demand for—his work. And now Pensamientos Febriles II is about to open in Berlin. Be prepared for art world fireworks!"

———

A glamorous TV reporter at an ultramodern gallery in Berlin previewed the exhibition, which was about to open. "No one has seen Ricardo Casa DeSpiritu. He is a complete enigma. Amparo Terrasombra nurtured his meteoric rise. She claims he is a recluse.

"Amparo serves as his connection to the world. She says Ricardo has no desire to meet the public at this time. Accordingly, Amparo has not provided his biography. She says he is less than forty years old. Amparo begs for understanding of his state of mind and asks the press not to try to find him. She fears exposure to the public eye would disturb his incredible, creative energy.

"It seems that Herr DeSpiritu is expressing the inner energy of a troubled—perhaps convalescing—psyche. We have studied paintings in this exhibition and compared them to his exhibition in Mexico City two months ago. Though always deep and out of reach for complete aesthetic dissection, his new works are more energetic and colorful. They suggest readiness to evolve from a constrained message to one of greater personal freedom.

"All forty-five works in this exhibition will be up for auction—and yes, dear art lovers, a Ricardo Casa DeSpiritu does not come cheap. Starting bids on all works will be fifty thousand euros.

"But not to worry, if his paintings are a little high. You can have a Ricardo-Casa-DeSpiritu-endorsed product at a price closer to what your pocketbook allows. The market-savvy Amparo is selling T-shirts, hats, and leather goods at the exhibition. You can even buy her tequila for two hundred euros a bottle."

The reporter continued, "Amparo is a master at bringing out new products at lightning speed—in this supercharged world of contemporary art."

Chapter 23

GROUND ASSETS AT WORK

Puerto Rana Verde is nestled behind a long breakwater—a dredged inlet links the well-protected lagoon to the open sea. Old quays of concrete, cracked and spalled, berthed the larger vessels. Motley, old fishing boats were moored between floating docks and pilings leaning in every direction. On the harbor's north side, entering from the ocean, was a newer berth displaying a large black, white, and red sign: EL CAPITAN NEMO—SUBMARINO DE EXCURSIÒN.

A sign on a small building at the dock entrance offered tickets for cruises of one or two days. French Scientist stood at the ticket window. He wore khaki shorts, a floppy hat, high, lace-up shoes, and a grimy wife-beater. He inquired how deep the submarine dove and what kind of creatures it found at different depths and locations.

An attendant showed him oceanographic maps of the area. A binder of interior photos featured generous viewing windows for the eight customers that made up a typi-cal excursion.

Surfers were riding paddleboards around the harbor and cruising the girls when they took a swim.

Taco Vendor wheeled his cart between the harbor and its gravel parking lot. A compartment in his cart had limpet transponders shaped like silver dollars that attached to vehi-cles by magnetism. They put out a beacon signal for remote tracking. To his annoyance, an American couple ordered ta-cos, which he was not very good at making.

Back in the JOC, screens displayed video images from the Taco Vendor's and Surfer's special cell phones, giving the JOC team a good understanding of the harbor layout and appearance.

Tourist Couple was sitting in a convertible eating tacos. They were waiting for instructions from JOC through their hearing aid radios, when the thrumming of diesel engines her-alded El Capitan Nemo's return. It was an odd-looking vessel from the age of iron and rivets—suiting its namesake. Three men stood on deck ready to handle mooring lines. Eighty-feet long and well maintained—at least there were no visible rust spots or oil slicks emanating from the hull—it nestled up to pier bumpers and stopped. Mooring lines were thrown to the pier attendants, and a gangplank was put in place.

Four men came out of the conning tower door. They walked over the gangplank—drawing intense scrutiny at the JOC screens. The JOC team recognized Fidel Terrasombra right away, as he walked along the pier. The other three men with him were thought to be crewmembers. JOC signaled ground assets to stay close to Fidel, who was wearing a black hat.

Before he got into the waiting black Ford Explorer, Fidel and the three men from the sub went into the beach bar. The driver of the Explorer waited outside for him. Reacting quickly, Surfers filed into the bar soon after. They start knocking back tequila shooters and linking Fidel's image and conversation back to a JOC screen from their cell phones. A subtitled translation of Fidel telling his companions "At Spring Break this place is just jumping with pussy" appeared on the bottom of the screen. Uproarious laughter burst out at the JOC.

"All right, keep it down," barked the commander.

JOC commands directed Taco Vendor to the Explorer's rear to attach a limpet inside its bumper.

"How about a tour of the submarine?" asked French Scientist at the submarine booth.

The attendant said, "OK, boss, follow me. I'll take you inside." French Scientist saw for himself the control room, bunk areas, and a windowed compartment for undersea viewing. The attendant switched on brilliant lights, used to attract fish in dark waters. Fascinated as he was with its capabilities, French Scientist hadn't forgotten his main mission, furtively attaching limpets in different places.

Tourist Couple ordered a few more tacos and waited for Fidel to leave. When he eventually drove away, they followed ten miles behind—guided by JOC tracking the Explorer by satellite. Seven hours later the Explorer headed off the highway onto an unpaved road.

———

JOC command, now knowing the destination was near, ordered Tourist Couple to stop in a location where they would not be seen and to release the drone and two spy bots for the kind of high-image resolution that the satellite couldn't provide.

Tourist Couple pulled off the desolate highway and satisfied themselves that no cars were approaching for miles in either direction. Then Tourist Man took the drone that looked like a model airplane with a three-foot wingspan from a plastic case in the trunk. Tourist Man switched it on, starting its propeller, and launched it with a smooth, upward throwing motion and turned control from his iPad over to the JOC operators. It was amazingly light but fast enough to catch up with Fidel's Explorer as it entered the hacienda. It then went into orbit a mile above it.

With iPad control Tourist Lady guided the Bird Bot in a similar way and turned it over to JOC control at tree top altitude. Tourist Man then switched on the lowly Spider Bot and aimed it down the edge of the highway under JOC control.

Tourist Couple then searched the Internet for a hotel while awaiting the next assignment from the JOC.

Chapter 24

THE END IS NEAR

With a week to go on the painting, Mitch woke up before dawn—oddly, without a real nightmare to erupt out onto a canvas. It was his habit to get up and paint, so he looked around for a subject. Ah! His sandals were lying by his bed. What the hell? Great artists, from Van Gogh to Bongart, had painted old shoes. His turn now.

He imagined comic titles for the picture: *Sandals to Nowhere, Huarache Happiness, Nothing Like the Smell of Sandals in the Morning.* Grabbing brushes and paints set up the night before in anticipation of a Dream Wreck, he jumped in with his usual rapid-fire brush action. Painting *alla prima* with no looking back. Just about halfway through, it hit him: a way to escape!

Near the sandals he noticed a bed construction feature that could be his passport to freedom—the bed sideboard, about which his chain was looped, was mortised into the headboard. If he could force that joint apart, the chain could be slipped off, and he could escape—albeit with twenty pounds of chain to carry with him. For weeks he had decided that he would go over the wall to escape and had worked out a plan for every detail, except one thing: how to free himself from the chain. Now he had a way around that last obstacle. Just had to try it out without being noticed by anyone.

He slid a wastebasket just under the edge of his bed near the joint to be separated.

Confident no one was watching, he turned the light off and applied force to the headboard with his feet by straightening his legs. The sideboard pulled out of the headboard and dropped down an inch, landing on the wastebasket instead of falling farther and making noise.

He quickly replaced it. Couldn't concentrate on painting sandals then—too much going on in his head. He lay down, knowing that he could detach the sideboard again for escaping. His heart took a leap. *Got my ticket to freedom!*

He went over his escape plan: Once out of the bathroom window, he would use a couple of boxes and wastebaskets from the adobe for climbing props to pull himself up and over the wall. He would throw bed covers over the broken glass on top. From then on it would be escape-and-evade tactics for about ten miles to reach the highway, far from the hacienda turnoff. Basic stuff for a marine. It had been years since he'd tested himself to such a distance, but he was confident he could make it, as the gently rolling terrain wouldn't present extreme obstacles. Just had to take enough water to trek across it for twelve hours at the most. His escape would take place about 4:00 a.m.—quietest time in the hacienda. Hector, on the main house veranda, was asleep in his chair at this time and wouldn't notice him anyway climbing out the back window with his adobe lights off.

———

The sun was coming up, and his thoughts turned to Amparo. The anticipation of her visits became everything in his life. Her posing for him was a joy, and the chance to help her find the pose with a touch on her shoulder was icing on the cake. He mused, *What a sneak I am! At every session I find something about her pose to be adjusted—my excuse to touch her.*

But now it was coming to an end—the end of the furtive touches, the abrazos, the being near but not able to speak one's heart. Glances, grins, smiles, frowns, and just being in the same room, he realized now, kept him hoping, kept him sane.

He knew then that he was deeply in love.

They would be together when he got out, or he would die trying. War taught him to face danger with determination and with every ounce of his inner strength. He would face mortal danger just a week away. If he survived, he would have a chance for pure happiness. And he was ready.

With morning light coming into the studio, he surveyed the big canvas. *Sort of looks like a John Singer Sergeant family portrait,* he thought and smiled. *Dark background with La Señora off center to the right, in the ornate chair. Fidel and Maximilliano flanked her. Amparo, farther back on the left, is the only one not looking toward the viewer.*

He grinned as he thought that the critics would say she looks toward La Señora in respect for her as matriarch. But that wasn't the reason. Amparo looking straight ahead in the painting would mean she would have to pose looking into his eyes as he painted. No way he could handle that, especially now with his pressure cooker of pent-up emotions ready to blow.

Panchito unlocked him and went to pick up breakfast. Mitch washed, dressed, and sized up the week ahead. *Just a little work to do on all the faces and then add a few highlights and dark passages on everyone's clothing. I'll stretch the few hours' work needed into a week. That week ends with Amparo's last pose here. Not enough to keep me busy, but I won't crack up—even if I have to do five hundred push-ups a day to use up the adrenaline.*

He thought a lot about escaping in the coming week but had no opportunity of telling this to Amparo during her last visit—always somebody around watching and listening to them as she posed. *If I just disappear, it could wreck everything,* he thought. *She would come here and I would be gone, without saying goodbye, just before finishing her face in the painting. She likes me and is looking forward to the last posing session. I'm afraid if I'm gone when she shows up this weekend it would disappoint her—maybe destroy her confidence in me. Can't do that. Gotta be here. I'll go over the wall after the painting is done.*

———

Panchito returned and set a large tray on the patio table and started unloading it.

"We got *chorizo* sausage, eggs, papaya, cinnamon rolls, coffee." Not seeing the usual Dream Wreck in progress, Panchito chuckled and said, "Huaraches today, a new painting subject for you?"

Mitch replied with a laugh, "Painting shoes means I am ready to travel."

They sat down together, and Panchito said, "Enjoy your meal."

"Thanks, Panchito."

"Been watching your morning abstractos, Mitch. Don't know much about that kind of art, but everyday I see a little change, something new and different."

Mitch, surprised to hear that Panchito was observing his progress, asked, "Do you think they are getting better?"

Panchito took a slug of coffee, wiped his considerable moustache, and replied, "Could be. I think your first ones were like a bullfighter drawing a bad bull and not being able to display his ability. They were full of action but dark—not too steady. Now your abstractos have more color. There are more definite lines in them, like a bullfighter making confident, graceful passes."

"An elegant description," said Mitch—liking Panchito's analogy.

Panchito responded with an embarrassed chuckle.

"Someday after I am finished here at the hacienda I would like to go to the Mexico City bullring with you," said Mitch, trying to tease out some information about his future.

"That would be nice," said Panchito, nodding his head slightly and then looking down into his coffee cup.

Chapter 25

BIRD BOT

Amparo drove in fast and parked at the studio door. "*Buenas tardes*," she said, greeting Panchito, who was sitting outside reading his paper. She gave him a bottle of Ricardo Casa DeSpiritu tequila before entering. Mitch was finishing a morning Dream Wreck—a tortured, splattered effort featuring the word *help* that was disappearing with his repeated splashes of clashing color.

He took it off his easel, leaned it against the wall, and replaced it with the family portrait.

"Before you start painting me, you must know that Berlin was *estupendo*!" Amparo exclaimed and gave him a giant abrazo. "We made a fortune on both paintings and merchandise."

"What merchandise?" said Mitch.

"I have franchised our Ricardo Casa DeSpiritu brand for use on everything from T-shirts to tequila. I don't totally understand it, Mitch, but people are going crazy to get their hands on anything associated with my mysterious Ricardo. You are rich."

"Rich?" Mitch took advantage of this rare moment—just two of them in the studio, with Panchito and Hector smoking on the patio. "Not sure I want to be rich, Amparo."

"What do you mean?" She was taken aback.

"My first goal is to stay alive. You see, the family portrait will be done in two days—then El Jefe has arranged for Hector and Raul to drive me to the airport.

"I am not sure I'll make it to the airport. Having a lot of money is not my first priority."

"Oh Mitch, what do you…?"

"I don't know anything a hundred percent, but I am not going to sit around and let it happen to me."

"I don't understand. I thought you were happy here," said Amparo, deeply concerned.

"Can I trust you?" asked Mitch.

Tears started streaming down her face. "How can you say that?" She was angry. "I've devoted the past four months to your success and happiness. I could see the anguish in your Dream Wrecks, and I could see them changing, with color coming in the recent ones. I could see you bring out the character in the portraits; that told me you too have deep emotions. I've been waiting for your response to my deep feelings—my attachment to you."

Mitch was putting out paint and preparing his brushes. He trembled at seeing her tears, hearing her say that, but fought off a reaction by clenching his jaw. Taking a deep breath to compose himself, he started adding touches to her face in the portrait. Still painting, he said softly, "Amparo, Panchito and Hector are watching as they always do. I want you to get into your pose and try to look happy. Let me talk without raising their suspicion."

"OK, Mitch, I'll try," she said, still upset. She dabbed her eyes and stood in the spots marked on the floor for her feet.

Trying to cheer herself up, she said, "*Mira*, a little bird has just flown to the windowsill."

Speaking softly, just loud enough for her to hear, Mitch said, "Amparo, I am not a guest here. I am a prisoner. I was kidnapped and taken here to paint La Señora's portrait."

Amparo's eyes widened, and she gasped, "Oh no!" But she remained still.

Mitch continued, "I asked La Señora to convince El Jefe she needed a family portrait, so I could drag out my stay another two months. Needed time to figure a way out."

"Oh my God," she said, "and now it's almost done."

"Under my bed is a chain that Panchito attaches to my ankle every night so I won't escape. I have been told El Jefe is very protective of you, so I have been very careful when you are here. To those living here and watching me, I can be friendly to you but can't for a minute seem closer than that… They're coming. Gotta stop talking."

Panchito and Hector stepped into the studio to watch him at work. Panchito said, "It is beautiful, almost done. I'll be getting lunch while Hector keeps you company."

After Panchito left, Hector stood with his usual dour expression, watching Mitch carefully add finishing touches to Amparo's face. Then he said, "Artista, Raul, and me, we take you to the airport in two days. You don't have to pack nothing. I send your stuff to you."

Amparo fought back a worried expression and struggled to hold her pose.

Mitch said flatly, "Thanks, Hector. You've thought of everything."

Hector turned and walked outside to smoke.

Amparo suddenly said, "I can't pose any longer. I've got to get to the city. I've got to think of something…" Seeing Hector just outside the door, she stopped speaking. Abruptly, she gave Mitch a quick, tense hug and left.

———

He flopped onto his bed. Seeing her sad at leaving depressed the hell out of him. That old pressure on his chest came back, after a long absence. A torrent of thoughts fought it out in his mind—none of them good ones. They exhausted him, bringing sleep, until Panchito woke him up for dinner.

Mitch stood up, feeling groggy, stretched, and walked to the patio table where he and Panchito had shared meals for the past four months.

"Fish tonight and beers," said Panchito, setting plates of Veracruz style grilled mahi mahi down for both of them.

Great food, shitty life, Mitch thought. He suppressed a sardonic half grin and said, "Life is good. Salud." They clinked their beer glasses and dug in.

Panchito amiably described the latest bullfighting sensation in Mexico City. He was one of two brother bullfighters from Spain. He had fought a brilliant fight the previous weekend and had been awarded both ears of the fallen bull. Panchito, a lover of the *corrida*, went on to tell of the great bullfighters he had seen, going back to El Cordobés. At times like this, Mitch enjoyed his company because Panchito told long, enjoyable stories that required only an occasional word or short question from Mitch—who wasn't in the mood for talking.

The tales of the corrida went on for an hour. When Mitch started nodding off while trying to listen, Panchito said, "Buenas noches, Amigo." And a little later, he locked the leg iron.

Chapter 26

JOC ON ALERT

Commander Heartworthy and her JOC team were totally focused on a screen labeled FINCHCAM. At her command, a drone controller maneuvered Bird Bot around the hacienda. They tried various vantage points until they found Mitch's studio windowsill with its well-lit view of an artist at work. He was painting his model on a large canvas when Bird Bot flew up.

Quickly checking their FINCHCAM artist image against the missing artist's reference photos, they knew they had a match: Mitch Alexander.

There he was, working on a large painting. Seemed to be in good physical shape, too. The JOC was abuzz with this surprising development. Then the commander ordered total silence.

On FINCHCAM, all hands were watching and hearing the studio events unfold—starting when Amparo remarked,

"Mira, a little bird has just flown to our windowsill. It's watching us."

When Mitch said he was a prisoner, the commander suppressed a startled breath and then said over the JOC intercom network, "We're coming, Mitch; hang in there."

Silence from all—until they heard Hector say, "Artista, Raul, and me, we take you to the airport in two days. You don't have to pack nothing, I send your stuff to you." Gasps were heard in the JOC.

Commander Heartworthy realized Mitch might be facing death in two days. She didn't see anything to be gained by El Jefe in letting him go. She only saw a threat to El Jefe if the artist revealed what he knew after four months as a prisoner.

The commander jumped to her feet and turned to those seated behind her who had also been watching the studio drama in stunned silence. "Teammates, we are going to rescue Mitch Alexander, or he could be killed the day after tomorrow." She ordered CIA agents to position ground assets at several locations near the hacienda.

A voice came up on the net: "Commander Heartworthy, we have a positive ID on the woman posing for Mitch Alexander. She is Amparo Terrasombra, a niece of El Jefe."

"Ten four," replied the commander. "She does not appear to be complicit in the scheme to terminate the artist. We will not surveil her."

"Roger that."

The commander asked the Bird Bot controller, "Can you get a look at the painting Alexander is working on?"

"Think so." Minutes later, the controller said, "Got it now, with Bird Bot at the front window of the adobe. It is a group portrait of El Jefe, his brother Fidel, an elderly lady, and Amparo.

"Looks like they kidnapped Alexander to paint the family."

Chuckles.

Commander Heartworthy got offline to confer in private with her top advisors. After ten minutes, she said over the JOC intercom: "Teammates, here's the plan. When Hector's vehicle leaves the gate in two days and is out of range of hacienda armaments, we will interdict that vehicle to liberate Mitch Alexander.

"We have a stealth drone overhead now. Between it and Bird Bot, we will surveil all vehicular movements for the next two days. We'll know when his vehicle drives out the gate."

JOC team members were all glued to surveillance screens. They would be on station in shifts until conclusion of the operation. The mood was deadly serious. Drone imaging revealed little movement at the hacienda that night, except for Amparo's vehicle driving south. As ordered, the team did not pursue it further.

Satellite electromagnetic radiation sensors detected no phone calls or online transmissions to or from the hacienda. Bird Bot and Spider Bot had accounted for everyone in the hacienda by peering in windows and doors.

Dudley Henshaw asked, "Are you conductin' this operation in cooperation with Mexican authorities?"

Commander Heartworthy replied, "No, not initially."

"Why not? This could become an international incident."

"We are concerned about leaks in the Mexican government and will keep it an all-American operation. We will be demonstrating that we can outsmart international gangsters with a coordinated effort of Homeland Security, FBI, CIA, navy, and NSA assets. We have never had this level of cooperation before. I might add we have never reached this level of technological finesse either. You have witnessed everything from our infiltrated assets to satellites, drones, and robot birds—all flawlessly coordinated here in the JOC. The Mexican authorities are notoriously leaky, full of narco moles. We might endanger our own people if narco moles leak who they are.

"We leave a small footprint in Mexico—after rescuing Mitch Alexander, he will be driven back home in a van full of Surfers—actually US Navy Seals. Only after he is back in the United States do we release Hector and Raul on a back road in Belize.

"The main objective of this team naturally is to take down El Jefe's cartel. We will, of course, notify Mexican authorities of El Jefe's presence at the hacienda and his submarine. Then we will turn over everything we have on El Jefe's US operations and arrest all his people in the United States—after Mitch Alexander's rescue."

Dudley asked, "You tellin' the president about this operation?"

"After we rescue Mitch Alexander and are working in cooperation with the Mexican authorities, we'll elevate the visibility of this operation to the highest levels."

Dudley replied, "Ah wish ya luck."

Chapter 27

SOUL SEARCH

Driving out of the hacienda gate, Amparo felt a dark cloud of anxiety settle over her, her shoulders tensed and her grip on the steering wheel tightened. Short of breath, she anguished as she thought, *Never will they kill him—I'll do everything I can to stop them!*

Composing herself, she took a deep breath and thought, *I've got to stop Tio Max.* Her car rumbled over the gravel road toward the highway to Mexico City. She passed a side road that led to the inactive Lopez Quarry. At the highway she turned right, passing a larger sign that read: "La Cantera Lopez."

Traffic was light. Traveling fast, she turned on some un-winding music—as she usually did after a grinding day at the gallery. Debussy's impressionistic tones softly surrounded her as she thought, *Time for me to grow out of a child's view of my uncle—should have chucked that baggage a long time ago. Now I hate him so much I could kill him myself.* She switched the music off—didn't suit her raw feelings.

I denied the stories about his ruthlessness and power. How could I have been so blind? she thought. It was too easy to go on thinking that he, who opened doors to schools, tickets, choice tables, and jobs, was a loving uncle—and to let his veil of protection lie lightly on her shoulders. It was comfortable to close her mind, opting for a reflected share of a malevolent power. She stuck up for her family, right or wrong. *I told a lot of people that. Or I told them everyone with a lot of money has skeletons in the closet.*

She had heard he was chasing off any guy who showed an interest in her—and the word was out there. Seemed every Mexican man knew about that threat and steered clear of her. *Yes, I heard these stories, but that didn't bother me during my climb to success in the art world—didn't have time for steady dating anyway.* She used to delude herself that a lot of men weren't ready for a successful woman. The machismo thing. That was OK while working twelve-hour days and weekends. She could keep totally focused on work.

So she didn't worry about Tio Max's threat to interested men. Shrugged it off because she knew she would find her own man someday—not one that Tio Max would pick for her. But that was way out there in the future. Amparo knew there would be a time when she turned her drive for success in the world toward love and the fulfillment of a family of her own.

It just happened sooner that she thought!

It was happening then. Mitch was it. Destiny dropped him there at the hacienda. Tears slipped out of her eyes as she visualized him chained in his adobe. *I hate you, Tio Max, you rotten devil!*

All she could think of doing was to report Tio Max to the government. The new president of Mexico was arresting drug lords. If Amparo got him arrested at the hacienda, his gang would fall with him, and Mitch would be freed.

Amparo knew she couldn't reveal that she reported him—what was left of his gang would kill her. Even members of the Terrasombra family, who were not criminals but outraged about this act of betrayal, could do her harm. A lot of them, like her, basked in the glow of Tio Max's influence. They wouldn't be comfortable being on their own. *But so be it,* she thought. *I'm fighting for my future and the life of the man I love. I am not giving anyone a free shot at me, either.*

Pulling into a shopping mall south of Querétaro, Amparo bought a prepaid cell phone. Dropping into an Internet café, she contacted a phone company website in India. The contact there took the International Mobile Equipment Identity (IMEI) number she read off the phone, keyed in the false name and address she provided, and created a phone number based on the area code for the shopping mall.

Another fifty miles toward Mexico City, Amparo turned off the highway into a soccer-stadium parking lot. Scared but determined she dialed information for the drug enforcement hotline. Had to be a short call. Narco moles in the government could trace her location and find her sitting in her car—if she stayed on the line too long. She didn't know how much time she had but decided to keep the call less than five minutes.

A voice answered, "Bueno, Narcotics Enforcement Hotline."

Amparo spoke through a scarf over her mouth to disguise her voice. "I want to give you the exact location of Maximilliano Terrasombra, and I want him arrested."

"How do I know you are telling me the truth?"

"The hacienda where he is located is off of Highway 111 on the south side. There is a turnoff near the sign to La Cantera Lopez about nineteen kilometers west of the intersection with Highway 57. Continue on the turnoff road past the quarry entrance for four kilometers. There is a walled hacienda there. There are about seven or eight security people armed with pistols. His mother lives there now and receives mail there. El Jefe is an occasional visitor."

"Have you personally seen him there?"

"Two hours ago I saw him there. I know Maximilliano will be there until Monday morning."

"How often does he come to this location?"

"No telling, he moves continually on a random basis—you must get him before he leaves the day after tomorrow, in the early morning."

"Why so urgent?"

"There is a life at stake," said Amparo, sounding frustrated.

"Whose?"

"Can't tell—could endanger that person."

"Is Maximilliano armed?"

"I don't know. I have seen gun racks in his game room."

"Señora, now tell us something about yourself."

"For God's sake, you must do something."

She hung up, started her car, and drove off.

The telephone smashed on the highway after she threw it out the window.

Chapter 28

FAMILY PORTRAIT IS DONE

Waking early, Mitch rambled about the studio until Panchito unlocked his chain. The little bird flew up and perched on the windowsill again, as it had for long periods of time since yesterday. Mitch was keyed up, determined to break out that night or die trying.

Last night with lights out, he practiced getting the bed sideboard loose and the chain out and looped around his waist and shoulders—ready for traveling. He was ready for the night ahead.

Panchito had treated him well, and Mitch liked him, even though Panchito was totally loyal to El Jefe. But it was crunch time now. If it came down to choosing between Panchito and freedom, Mitch knew he would have to take Panchito out. No one was going to block his way over the wall. Hector was another story, whacking him or choking him with the chain was something he would look forward to.

A late breakfast with Panchito—then Mitch signed the family portrait with his *nom de art*, Ricardo Casa DeSpiritu, and pressed a thumbprint on the side of the canvas. It was done.

Maximilliano and Fidel waited for La Señora to come out of the little chapel after mass. She appeared still wearing her mantilla and carrying her prayer book. Padre Francisco was at her side. The four talked for a few minutes then Padre Francisco headed for his old VW, leaving La Señora and her sons to stroll to the studio to see the final work.

Upon entering, La Señora exclaimed, "Mitch, you have done your magic again! You have put three people that I love most in this world together with me. May God bless your hands that did this work."

"Mil gracias, Señora."

Fidel said, "I knew you could do this from the first day I met you, when you painted my portrait in an hour."

"You are definitely a man of good taste, Señor Fidel." Mitch strived for joviality. "Glad you like it."

El Jefe extended his hand, and Mitch shook it. "Goodbye, Mitch. Hector and Raul will come for you after breakfast tomorrow."

A shiver went up Mitch's spine as he replied, "Good-bye, Señor Maximilliano."

La Señora and her sons filed out of the studio.

———

Mitch needed to stay busy to keep his mind focused and on a positive arc. He carefully cleaned his brushes in mineral spirits, and then cleaned them again with soap and water. Scraped and cleaned his palette and easel. Still looking for things to do, he squeezed tubes of paint to get all the contents near the top.

He stacked his sketchbooks and watercolor gear on a worktable. Then arranged the mahl stick, remaining art supplies, and small supply of clean clothes there too. He was acting out how he would be preparing for someone to come tomorrow to pack his stuff and send it to LA—as Hector said he would. This careful preparation was a charade: having everyone believe he was getting ready to go home and that he was not onto the fate that actually awaited him.

But he found it comforting in a way, cleaning and stacking everything. Ending one chapter of his life in preparation for beginning the next one.

He was glad his obligation to finish the paintings was fulfilled—brought a sense of accomplishment. He was pleased with the outcomes of the two major works, because he had never worked so much before on serious paintings. *Amazing, what I can do with my life at stake!* he thought. Relaxed and in a state of mental alertness, he was quietly storing resolve and psychic energy for the hours ahead.

Nothing to do now. I'll just sit outside and soak up the end of another day of blue skies and tumbling clouds competing for space above the hacienda. He decided not to read *Treasure of Sierra Madre* for the third time. Instead he'd just sit until dinner.

Panchito brought dinner for one. Said he wasn't feeling well enough to eat. Mitch started to eat while Panchito knocked back shots of Ricardo Casa DeSpiritu tequila and sat silently. Mitch thought they brought him his favorite dish, *tacos de carnitas*, because a condemned prisoner always gets his favorite request for his last meal.

That's OK; let 'em think that. He ate slowly, thoughtfully, with just one beer. *Got to stay sober.* He took coffee and savored the rum cake afterward.

"Hey, Panchito, this is my going-away party," he joked.

He got a wan smile and a chuckle in return.

Chapter 29

THINGS CHANGE

Panchito locked the leg iron without saying much and disappeared out the door about midnight. Mitch was ready to burst
out—never clearer, never more focused. He knew sleeping for
a few of hours would be impossible—before freeing the chain,
wrapping it around his waist and shoulders, climbing out the
rear window, and sneaking over the wall.

Mitch lay in bed thinking about his last four months
in Mexico. Not a bad studio, plenty of supplies, and three
squares a day. During times when he got out to buy supplies,
he soaked up the great scenery on the high plateau with its
endless vistas and distant mountains. Sudden thunderstorms
were a treat for a guy from LA—where they hardly ever happen. But the end-game reality was inescapable, it lurked in his
consciousness much of the time.

Dream Wreck painting he had down to a one-hour
routine—plenty of time left in the day for painting on the two
big works or dabbling with watercolors or still lifes. Didn't

have to work too hard. After all, he prolonged the big paintings, going slowly as he played for time.

Then Amparo came into his life. Her class and poise overpowered him at first. Mitch was just starting to climb out of a marginal life, banging out Dream Wrecks to make it through the day, he was trying to get a grasp on things, when he got snatched and brought here, way south of the border.

Amparo was way beyond trying to get a grasp on things— she had a grasp on a lot of things. Successful in her Mexico City gallery. International player in the art world. Educated from the best nun's schools to the best fine art and business schools.

His initial feeling of awe changed with her visits to his studio. He became less awed and more comfortable with her, as she showed an unstinting generosity on his behalf—that to him meant she was 100 percent behind him and his work. That total openheartedness on her part beckoned to him to open his heart to her—to forget the awe, to be a friend.

Lying there looking at the dark ceiling, he started to daydream about her and about staying down in Mexico to be close to her. Then daydreams changed into more intimate scenarios that went beyond beginning love to sensual fulfillment.

She knew how to wear expensive clothes that showed off a gorgeous figure without being really obvious. Didn't have to be any more obvious for his temperature to rise when she visited. He wondered if her light caramel complexion was that smooth and vibrant all over her body.

What did she think about him? He thought her friendship for him had turned in the direction of love. But was it as intense and obsessive as his love for her? Lying there in darkness, his mind imagined Amparo walking in and seeing him in bed—lying down alongside him. Then she kissed him deeply. Her smooth silk blouse was easy to unbutton and then…

Kaboom! An explosion, real close. *Another friggin' nightmare, but man—loudest nightmare I've ever had.* He heard more explosions, shouting in Spanish, automatic rifle fire, sounds of running footsteps.

Shit! This isn't a nightmare; it's real. *Gonna look out and see what's going on.*

Mitch sat up in bed just as his door was kicked open; a bright light shone in his eyes. He squinted, making out soldiers with guns pointed at him. "*Manos Arriba*! Hands up. Come outside!"

Standing up, Mitch raised his hands and walked, dragging his chain as far as it would go, then he had to stop. "I'm a prisoner here!" he yelled, voice quavering. "Can't ya see I'm dragging a chain?"

A captain, Salazar on his nameplate, turned a studio light on and told his men to back off. He asked Mitch, "What are you doing here?"

"I was kidnapped in California by El Jefe's gang and brought here to paint a portrait of his mother. Been captive four months."

"You expect me to believe that?" asked Capitan Salazar.

"Yeah, look at that painting. It didn't paint itself," said Mitch, pointing at the family portrait.

"No time for jokes, Gringo," said Capitan Salazar menacingly.

"I am more civil without a chain on my leg," said Mitch.

The captain commanded a soldier, "Chucho, shoot that lock off his chain."

"Whoa!" yelled Mitch. "Hold on; he could hit my foot."

"Chucho," said the captain with a sly grin.

"Sí, Capitan."

"Shoot that bird."

Chucho immediately raised his rifle and shot the gold finch perched on the windowsill, blowing it to pieces. "He never misses," said Capitan Salazar. "Now sit down and hold your leg out so the lock is hanging down." Mitch sat in a chair, held his leg out, and covered his face against shrapnel.

The captain motioned to Chucho, who raised his rifle, blowing away the lock. The leg iron fell off. The captain ordered, "Soldiers report to Lieutenant Gil. I will be here for twenty minutes to question our artista."

He turned to Mitch and said, "Gringo, get dressed and let's talk."

Chapter 30

RAUL ON BOARD

Raul drove to the hacienda from his Michoacán lair. He pulled up at the gate in a dark blue Ford Explorer in time for a late dinner with El Jefe, Fidel, and their mother. After dinner when El Jefe's mother excused herself for the night and Fidel had gone into town to meet friends, he and El Jefe went to the game room.

They talked at length about infiltrating US border defenses. El Jefe used every possible means of smuggling: motor vehicles at border-crossing points; human mules along thousands of miles of border; tunnels under the border; unmanned air vehicles; boats; submarines; and airline cargo. El Jefe's brain boys kept statistics on success rates of each method and selected a means of transportation for drug shipments based on a profit-optimizing methodology.

Raul had heard these self-glorifying stories before. El Jefe knew a lot, and Raul had learned much from him in recent years. But Raul knew something that El Jefe didn't—the government was going to raid the hacienda—that night. An army mole had sent the news in a secure message to Raul's Blackberry as he drove to the hacienda. He couldn't turn back. The drug world would be thinking he had something to do with setting El Jefe up. That would be his death sentence. El Jefe wouldn't know what was in store for him because his courier system was too slow.

Raul realized things might get a little hot but knew his chance for real power was at hand. When the shooting started, El Jefe wouldn't survive, and he would. Might be in jail for a short while. From there Raul knew he could still direct his boys to take over El Jefe's operation, and he could run it with an up-to-date communication network.

———

When the first explosions signaled the onset of the army's attack, Raul and El Jefe were still in the game room drinking brandy, smoking cigars, and playing pool. They grabbed AK-47s from a gun rack. Ran upstairs to the balcony. Taking up firing positions, they faced the troops running through the gate toward the main house. El Jefe shot a few bursts, drawing the soldier's attention and shots in return.

Now's my chance, thought Raul, shooting a burst into the side of El Jefe's head. *Just got to stay alive for the next ten minutes.* He bounded downstairs and stuck his AK-47 back in the rack. He lay on the floor hoping for protection from the thick adobe walls and a massive pool table between him and the game room door.

A flash of light and thunderous explosion stunned him. Out of his blurred vision, he began to see soldiers looking down at him. They pulled him up and smashed a rifle butt into his face, shouting, "Where's El Jefe?"

Through broken teeth and bloody lips, Raul yelled, "Upstairs on the balcony!"

They dragged him off, cuffed him, and led him to the circle of prisoners. Sitting on the ground with hands behind his back, Raul was hurting. Blood was trickling down his chin, but he was satisfied with the way things were going. Soldiers working him over earned street cred with the thugs he was with. No threat from that direction. El Jefe was dead. No threat from that direction, either.

Chapter 31

JOCSIDE

Commander Heartworthy's deputy, Lieutenant Commander Bill Summers, called her at midnight. He reported that their drone had picked up movement of Mexican Army vehicles heading north on the highway toward the hacienda. They would reach the hacienda turnoff road in half an hour.

"I'll be there in twenty minutes."

Jumping to her feet, Commander Heartworthy put on her operational dress uniform that hung by her bed for just such an emergency. Gunning her Porsche Boxter, she made it to El Segundo in record time and headed for LA Air Force Base.

She ran into the JOC, took the commander seat in time to see Mexican troops break in to Mitch's studio—via Bird Bot. She and her night-shift team were fully alert. They were transfixed by what was happening on various screens being fed by drone and robot sensors.

Most eyes were on the FINCHCAM screen when Chucho shot Bird Bot, turning it into static and snow. A collective groan rose from the JOC team. Commander Heartworthy felt a punch to her gut. She threw her laser pointer violently against the blank screen, screaming, "That fucking idiot killed Bird Bot!" But then, with face still red, she commanded, "Bring up our Spider Bot feed."

A minute later it was on screen, showing a very different picture from ground level. The hacienda was crowded with soldiers milling about. El Jefe looked dead as he was wheeled out on a gurney to an ambulance. Hector was lying in the dust, obviously dead. A dozen prisoners, including Panchito and Raul, were corralled together with hands behind their backs. La Señora came out of the main house with the help of a maid. She was wearing her mantilla and weeping.

Regaining her command presence, Commander Heartworthy said, "The Mexican Army got there first; our mission might be compromised. Bring up our on-ground rescue assets."

A screen illuminated, showing Surfers being handcuffed by Mexican soldiers. Their captain said, "You expect me to believe you were headed for the beach when it's six hundred kilometers behind you? I think you are in the drug business." Then he turned from the glum Surfers and barked out a command to search all surfboards. Soldiers begin destroying them with axes.

Dudley Henshaw drawled, "I'd say our mission is definitely taking on water."

After the ambulances left with the casualties, Spider Bot was directed to Mitch's studio. The door was ajar and the chain lying on the floor. No one was there.

At ten in the morning, Commander Heartworthy spoke, "Team, we fought a good fight; our integrated systems took us close to the goal.

"Several hours before we would have rescued the kidnapped artist, Mitch Alexander, Mexican forces arrived. They achieved their objective, liquidating El Jefe. Naturally we are pleased that our Mexican colleagues took him out. A significant victory for the war on drugs. In coordination with them, we will stamp out any remnants of the Terrasombra cartel in the United States.

"We have instructed Tourist Couple to remain in Mexico to investigate financial operations of the Terrasombra cartel. We do not want any surviving operations to continue to do business, especially in the United States.

"I believe Mitch Alexander will be OK—as the rescuers could see he was imprisoned. We will alert American Consulates in Mexico to be on the lookout for him, and we will check to see if he pops up back home in LA. We want to bring closure to his kidnapping.

"Our Surfers are still in custody in Mexico. We plan to exchange information on the narco submarine operations for their release. There will be a reduction in force size and most of you will go back to your commands tomorrow. This afternoon there will be a group picture followed by a party at Tooters in Manhattan Beach."

Commander Heartworthy wearily walked to her office realizing that the Admiral's star on her uniform was not as close as she thought a day ago. She sat down at her desk and dropped her head into her hands.

She noticed through her tears that a CIA report on Terrasombra family finances was in her in-box.

Chapter 32

THE DEAL

Mitch dressed in the shirt and jeans he had planned to wear for his escape. He had cash from Amparo in his pockets. The captain had been talking with the commander of the raid and now was standing just outside the studio door.

Mitch didn't want to go with the army. *Where will they take me?* he wondered. *To what? Public exposure? Interrogation? Confinement? They could just ship me home. Who knows what?*

He decided he was not going home. Not just yet.

I love Amparo, he thought. *I'm staying in Mexico—but out of sight. I must see her as soon as possible, without getting either one of us in trouble.*

The captain returned and said, "El Jefe was shot dead, as was one guard. El Jefe's mother is OK. Haven't found his brother Fidel. When did you see him last?"

Mitch said, "Yesterday afternoon he came here with Maximilliano and his mother to see the finished painting; I didn't see him after that."

"How did you get here?" asked the captain.

"I was painting by the ocean one day in Malibu, California, up on a cliff. Fidel invited me to his house down by the water. He served me a couple beers. Next thing I know, I woke up on some kind of boat," he said. "I was drugged until it reached Puerto Rana Verde, and then El Jefe's people drove me here to paint a portrait of El Jefe's mother. Capitan, that's about it."

"There is more than his mother in that painting."

"That is the second painting that I did here," Mitch explained. "El Jefe's mother liked her portrait so much she wanted me to do another with her sons and her niece in it."

"How long did it take to do both paintings?"

"Four months."

The captain didn't say anything. He just looked around the studio and studied the painting a bit, and with an unreadable expression on his face, he turned back to face Mitch.

Mitch, thinking his story was not getting through, tried another tack. "I've been in this adobe all the time I was here; there's not anything else I can tell you. But there is one thing I want to ask of you."

The captain asked, "What's that?"

"I want to get dropped off in San Miguel de Allende when you pull out today."

"That's out of my way," said the captain. "Can't do that."

"Here are few pesos for extra gas," said Mitch as he handed over one of the payments from Amparo.

Riffling through the bills, the captain said, "Get your things together. I'll be back in half an hour, and you will go to San Miguel."

149

When the captain returned, he pulled his vehicle up on the patio near the door. He came into the adobe and gave Mitch an army jacket and hat. Told him to wear it and sit in back out of sight. They left in the dark. The captain said he wanted to be back in five hours, in time to leave with his unit.

In San Miguel, Mitch told the captain he wanted an ordinary hotel within walking distance of the Jardín.

The captain said, "I remember one up above the center of town. It used to be the home of the actor Cantinflas." They found La Posada Ermita several blocks uphill from the Jardín and banged on its gate. A sleepy-eyed clerk let Mitch in and rented him a small suite with living room, bedroom, and bathroom. It was perched up behind the pool.

All right! thought Mitch. *The captain picked a good hotel. Looks like I got my money's worth. Hope the night clerk wasn't too curious about me moving in with just two pillowcases of belongings—but I'm not sweatin' it—that guy was asleep seconds after giving me the key.*

There was a small living room where he could paint. He left the pillowcase with art supplies by the couch. Dropped the other holding his clothes and his personnel gear on the chair in his new bedroom. *Got to contact Amparo soon as possible. Middle of the night now—I'll do it first thing in the morning.*

He flopped onto the bed and slept until late morning, albeit woken a few times by church bells and crowing roosters—not by a nightmare. After eating breakfast in the hotel's little dining room, he headed for the front desk to inquire where he could buy a cell phone. Wasn't far, just a few short blocks.

He walked down to the Telemex store and bought a phone and a prepaid chip. Walked a few more blocks to the Internet café by the Jardín. It was upstairs over a travel agency. About twenty people, mostly gringos checking their e-mail, were clicking away at the keyboards. He rented an hour of computer time for fifteen pesos and joined them.

He Googled "Amparo Terrasombra" and quickly found her gallery website. He sent a message through the site: "Call me *pronto*" and typed in his new cell phone number. He signed off as "skinny gringo."

———

He sat in the Jardín, shaded by the laurel trees to be inconspicuous—just thinking. Just thinking mostly about her. *Call me, Amparo! I'm going nuts waiting to hear from you. I know she will call. Should have called her last night. Right now I have to stay out of sight and figure things out.*

More Googling at another Internet café found a breaking-news item: Drug Lord Maximilliano Terrasombra Killed in Secret Hacienda Raid. It read: "Acting on a tip, Mexican forces raided a secluded hacienda north of Mexico City. Hector Perez, one of El Jefe's bodyguards, also killed. Narco suspect Raul Casteneda and surviving armed guards at the hacienda were arrested. Other workers were interviewed and released— as was his distraught mother. She was picked up by a relative."

No mention of an artist—thank Jesus!

And ominously, no mention of Fidel. Shit! Hope this doesn't mean the Mexicans are not after him. *I've got to be careful now,* he thought, *and assume Fidel is after me—he's gotta be, because I know about his place in Malibu, and I know about his submarine trips. He might even think I tipped off the army on El Jefe's presence at the hacienda.*

Chapter 33

AMPARO RETURNS

Amparo got up Sunday morning after a restless night. She was tortured by fear that someone would be injured or killed by the army when it moved in—if it moved in. She thought there was a good possibility it would act, in view of public demands for action against narco criminals—but then there was her doubt that the army would get on the road in time.

Could there be spies in the army that would warn Tio Max? Yes, that too was possible. The narcos' ears were everywhere.

She went to her gallery to keep busy because the hours of suspense were becoming unbearable. By tomorrow morning Mitch would live or die. A thought kept returning to her mind, *There must be something else can I do to make sure he lives.*

It was quiet in the closed gallery. Too quiet. She tried to bury herself in paperwork piled in her in-box, but her brain was thrashed by a storm of conflicting alarms. She didn't have a good feeling that Mitch would be saved. She had to do more. But what?

She tried harder to dig through letters to be answered, bills to be paid, solicitations from charities, hopeful artists wanting a shot...and then the phone rang.

She answered, "Buenos días, Galeria Amparo."

"Hello, Amparo?"

"Sí," said Amparo, still shuffling through paperwork.

"This is Raul Casteneda."

"Do I know you, Raul?"

"Not yet. Your Uncle Maximilliano recommended I meet you. Max and I are friends and business colleagues."

It felt like an electric jolt to the back of her neck. "Oh!" Amparo uttered, caught off guard. *Must think fast. Got to use this call.* But her words didn't come right away.

He asked, "Are you still there?"

"Yes..." she said and hesitated, trying to suppress her rage at hearing his voice.

"Hello?" he said to the silence on the line.

Finally she took a breath, found her emotional footing. "Are you the Raul that is taking the artist from the hacienda to the airport tomorrow?"

There was hesitation on Raul's part. "Uh yes. Hector and I will be sending him back to LA."

"Good, glad you called," Amparo said slowly, buying time. Then inspiration! "Tell me what airport, flight number, and time."

"Why?"

"I want to see the artist off."

"See him off?" asked Raul, sounding puzzled.

"Yes, we've become acquainted during his stay at the hacienda."

"OK, Amparo, I'll call you back with that information."

The words tasted rotten in her mouth when she said, "Thanks, Raul. I look forward to meeting you at the airport."

"Hasta mañana."

She put the phone down, shaking with anger. She fumed. *How dare Tio Max hand me off to a gangster—one of the killers that are supposedly taking Mitch to the airport! I hate Tio Max more than ever.* She thought she could drive a knife through his heart—both of their hearts. *I know that pig Raul won't call back. Pretty sure he won't, but if he does, it would be good news. I'd know Mitch is going to LA.*

Amparo dug into her paperwork with determination, trying to keep her mind off the events at the hacienda. It was impossible. The grim churning of thoughts about Mitch and the danger he was in kept surging to the forefront of her mind.

God! What else can I do? she thought as the day dragged into afternoon with the ruminating thoughts becoming ever bleaker. She knew she must do something more besides just waiting to see if the army would get there in time. And then it hit her! *I must be there! I will go to the hacienda tomorrow morning, getting there by seven. If the army hasn't done its job by then, I am confronting Tio Max and that scummy Raul myself. I am not going to let them kill Mitch. If they do, they will have to kill me too!*

———

Next morning she was off before light. Raul never called back. She didn't expect him to anyway. Mitch's fate was in the hands of Raul and Hector.

It was a grim two-hour drive—no stars and occasional fog. Approaching the hacienda turnoff road as the night was brightening into a gray dawn, she saw army vehicles and soldiers.

A soldier flagged her over and asked, "Where are you going?"

Amparo replied, "To the Terrasombra hacienda to visit my grandmother."

"Wait here," he said, motioning her to the side of the road.

The soldier talked briefly on his portable radio. "Remain here until further orders," he said sternly. She sat there behind the wheel, staring into the gloom of the gray dawn.

Half an hour later, three ambulances drove out the hacienda road and headed toward Querétaro. Breath was forced out of her lungs; tears flowed down her cheeks. Oh good Christ, don't let it be…

The soldier walked to her car, talking on his radio again. "You can proceed to the hacienda gate to pick up your grandmother."

"Oh, thank God she is OK!" Amparo gasped. "Can you tell me what happened here?"

"There was a raid to capture Maximilliano Terrasombra a couple of hours ago. That is all I can say."

Chapter 34

THE MORNING AFTER

When the army raided, Fidel was not at the hacienda. Earlier that evening, after dinner with Maximilliano, Raul and La Señora he drove to San Miguel to meet his narco pals. Fidel needed some party time after a long stay in California. What better atmosphere to trade stories, jokes, and lies than the smoke and murk of La Cucaracha—a favorite bar with the drug crowd, rowdy adventure seekers, Euro trash and alkies of all stripes. Too drunk to drive home, he slept at a drinking buddy's villa a couple blocks away. After getting up badly hungover, Fidel belted back a shot of tequila and flipped on the noon TV news.

Brutal words and images stunned his consciousness.

"Dios mio! Oh no! Maxi is dead," he wailed and flopped into a chair, tears streaming.

He watched breaking news coverage in disbelief—chaotic thoughts overwhelmed his mind. The announcer said, "This raid on a remote hacienda north of Mexico City, resulted from a tip by an unknown person. Oddly, five American men were apprehended near the hacienda during the raid. They claimed to be surfers and remain in custody..."

His attention focused like a glowing laser when he heard: "result of a tip." Who tipped off the government? For hours this story replayed many times—accompanied with surges of weeping, cursing, and swearing revenge by Fidel. With each account he agonized and searched for clues leading to a traitor.

The hacienda had been a place of refuge for El Jefe—a place to occasionally get away from demands of cartel business in Michoacán. He built the hacienda for his parents and didn't visit often—but savored the time spent there. The well-paid hacienda staff was comprised of long-time, loyal employees. Panchito, Hector and other guards proved loyal by fighting fierce battles alongside El Jefe during the years of his rise to domination.

El Jefe loved his mother dearly and acquiesced to her every need or desire. La Señora stayed at the Hacienda for most of the year. Accordingly, El Jefe built a little chapel there, so she could go to mass a couple times a week during her long visits.

El Jefe brought in Padre Francisco from a little village ten miles away to say mass. This village in turn benefitted from his beneficence in various ways, including a school lunch program, school uniforms, a soccer field, sports equipment, and computers. No reason for the Padre to betray his benefactor.

Fidel deduced that there was one person outside the circle of trusted employees and relatives at the hacienda: the gringo artist. He was guarded and kept close to his quarters except for a handful of times when Hector and Panchito took him to San Miguel for supplies. Could he have made contact with the CIA on these trips? Possibly.

Fidel had heard that the gringos had modern spy gear, even flying robots that looked like birds. No reason they couldn't figure out how to keep in touch with him. Peculiarities of the raid kept prying their way into his attention space, like the five so-called surfers. There were gringo surfers around the submarine dock when he landed. Same ones? Who the fuck knows? They all looked the same to him. TV images of soldiers wrecking their surf boards could have been an act to let Mexicans think that the surfers were just a bunch of assholes out to get stoned—while actually being CIA agents working with the Mexican government.

The government provided video coverage to the media that Fidel watched on TV for hours on end—but none of it showed the gringo artist. Poor Mamá led out crying, supported by a maid, brought tears to his eyes every time he saw it. Then the rest of the maids, chefs, and gardeners paraded out to a waiting school bus. He knew all of them to one degree or another and felt sad because their lives and incomes will be hard hit. The bodies of Maxi and Hector shown where they lay, and later shown wheeled out on gurneys, were heart-wrenching to see—causing him to sob uncontrollably and wail his torment out loud.

Fidel watched as the hacienda guards, sullen and cuffed, were displayed for the camera. Even a bandaged Panchito. Raul Casteneda was also displayed looking beat up. The TV commentator noted Raul was climbing higher in El Jefe's cartel management—but the government knew little about him.

Harsh images from the unending news coverage. The Army videos shown on TV served their purpose. They showed that El Jefe's soldiers were humiliated and no longer able to enforce Terrasombra power. Everyone else at the hacienda was shown on TV—but not the artist. Why, wondered Fidel? Maybe the government hid its gringo complicity with this successful raid because of Mexican sensitivity. Or maybe the army helped the CIA by not revealing one of its spies.

That hijo de puta! thought Fidel. *Son of a whore. Figured we couldn't let him go—even if he was just an artist. He knew too much. Always the danger of him revealing kidnaping, submarine, hacienda, Maxi, and...me.*

Maxi had been planning to get rid of him the next day. The artist must have figured out that he was done for. He must have called for help to escape and to take out El Jefe and me in the process. Fidel ended his rumination thinking, *Don't know exactly how he did it, but he tipped off our enemies. Now Maxi is dead and that fuckin' artist is going to die too. Because I am going to kill him.*

He turned off the TV—no sense pounding that horror story over and over into his roiling brain. Thinking further, he knew he would never get revenge unless he saved himself first. It was too dangerous in San Miguel, so close to the hacienda, crawling with soldiers. Too many people knew him. They could denounce him for a reward—or for settlement of an old grudge.

———

On the way out of town, he drove up past La Posada Ermita on the rough cobblestones—looking forward to the smooth roads that started on the outskirts of the city. He would hide out in a remote town along the coast called Playa Negra until things cooled down. People don't ask questions there—and don't mind if a stranger spreads some of his ill-gotten gains around. Clenching the steering wheel and staring straight ahead at the road to the west, Fidel thought about his dead brother. *I'll be back, Maxi. I'll get beyond this horrible day, and I'll be back to avenge you.*

Chapter 35

REUNION

Late in the afternoon following the raid, Mitch's new cell phone rang. "Bueno…Amparo?"

"*Gracias a dios.* Mitch, it's you!"

"Amparo," he replied with a thrill of excitement. "To hear your voice again…"

"Are you safe?" she burst in. "I can't talk long."

"I survived the fireworks OK," said Mitch, trying to be glib.

"Until I got your e-mail, I was afraid the worst happened," said Amparo, emotions rising.

Mitch said, "I'm in San Miguel de Allende…"

"Oh good! You're not far away…" Another pause and she started sobbing. "It's been awful; I feared you were hurt or killed in the raid."

"You must be going through hell, Mi Amor," he sympathized, "Can I call you that?"

"Always," replied Amparo fervently. "Always, Mi Amor."

"How can I help you?" Mitch said, wishing he could comfort her, "Don't cry. I want to…"

"TV, so terrible. Seeing them dead." More sobs. "Nothing about you. I thought you might be back in California."

"Couldn't do that. I had to stay. Have to see you."

"Stay here in Mexico, Mitch," she said, starting to calm down. "But you can't come where I am with the family. You have to stay out of sight."

"Amparo, can you come here?"

"In a week—after the funeral for Tio Max, I'll be there."

Mitch asked, "Does it have to be that long?"

"Mitch, you can't believe the state of the family. They are shocked and going crazy. They look to me to take care of final arrangements and everything else that comes along. No way I can get out of Morelia until after the funeral."

———

Mitch used his first week of freedom to get his life together. Took the bus to the giant market on Tuesday, Market Day. Routing through hundreds of stalls, he bought work clothes in gray and khaki—anything but his favorite blue denim, because that's how anyone from the hacienda would remember him. Bought a couple of suitcases to carry everything for the next move.

Riding the bus back to town, he was wearing a wide brim hat and sunglasses. Nonetheless, he was still concerned about being recognized.

In subsequent days he avoided walking the same streets every day. These evasions found him taking many routes through a beautiful city of cobblestone streets and colonial buildings. He soaked up the atmosphere of the city. The pace of everyday life, the color of aged masonry, cooking smells in the evenings. These things charged his senses with excitement—but never to the point of completely forgetting Fidel.

He figured Fidel was hiding from the authorities. Could be hiding anywhere in Mexico. Odds were against them both picking the same place. Fidel may even have taken a submarine trip back to California—where his face has not been seen in the newspapers and no one knew him.

But you never know.

Besides Fidel, he didn't want other El Jefe sympathizers to recognize him. Likewise, the Mexican Army and police might have an interest in talking to him or kicking him out of the country. One of the many Americans in town might recognize him from pictures in LA newspapers. *Wouldn't the press just salivate to get a scoop on me in Mexico? Sorry, guys, that's my story, and I'll tell it when I want. Until then, Amparo will be the only person to know my whereabouts.*

Mitch bought art supplies and a portable easel at El Gato, where he had been before. There was another art store a block from the Jardín, but it was too much in the middle of things for his comfort. He rationed his strolls through the lovely Jardín, so as not to become a remembered face.

Fidel could recognize him from that first portrait, when they looked into each other's eyes for an hour. With a good look into Mitch's face, Fidel's memory would recall facial details that don't change with a hat, a mustache, a shadow, or a haircut. He was hoping his new appearance wouldn't invite that first look into his face.

A gnawing desire for Amparo drove him. He channeled his excitement by painting distant vistas a few miles outside of town. San Miguel Tours arranged car and driver for these short trips. Remembering that the bad guys back in Malibu first saw him painting outside, he set up his easel out of sight of passing cars, and to the extent possible—passing people. San Miguel Tour drivers were good company, affable and helpful with his struggling Spanish.

Amparo called him most days, squeezing in short calls when time and privacy allowed. Her waking hours were full trying to keep La Señora and her relatives calm and directing final arrangements for her uncle. The family recognized her as the natural leader to handle things, especially now with Fidel disappeared in a flurry of wild theories about what might have happened to him.

Their calls were hurried and shorter than their two aching hearts desired. They knew that hours of face-to-face talking were still needed to fill in the knowledge of each other that the months of tantalizing and escalating love—without real communication—prevented.

His suite in the Posada La Ermita was starting to have a small collection of paintings and drawings from around San Miguel. Those distant vistas brought back the same sensation as the endless ocean. He surrendered his psyche to the great distances and the bluish horizon cutouts of the Sierra Madre Oriental Mountains.

He did morning paintings, though not exactly his Dream Wrecks that chronicled his tortured mind in the hacienda. Abstracts painted at dawn, but now with color, all kinds of unexpected color splattered and lathered on his canvases. Felt good to do them, like a quick morning workout.

While days were busy and full of color, people and new sights—nights were incredibly lonely. He used those dark hours to think of her and their lives ahead.

Finally she arrived.

———

The reunion days with Amparo were the happiest days of their lives. Both he—after trauma of war, mental illness, kidnapping—and she—after seeming success with girls' school, high-competition university and business environments—felt liberated, incredibly free, and intensely in love. Both were ready to surrender to a level of contentment that was new to them.

It started when Amparo drove up and checked into her suite at Posada La Ermita. She called Mitch. "Hola, Mitch, I'm ready for a glass of wine and dinner."

"When will you be here?"

"Already here—next door in fact."

A dark restaurant three blocks away yielded a corner table and space for the depths of feeling and private history they mined and traded. They flipped a coin to see who spoke first. Mitch won and revealed the story of his struggle. He told of the horror of war he had never told before, as well as a mental tapestry of fear and depression after coming back to California—and now his opening to contentment and hope.

She told of her privileged history with its constraints of family and religion. And she told of her obsession to succeed as a power in high-end international art. Then she told about meeting him at the hacienda and witnessing that freedom of an artist's heart. He was a man without a Rolex or tailored suit but was comfortable not wearing a watch at all, nor clothes that even fit right. A lot of hard-to-define things drew her to him; she had to keep coming back to spend a little time figuring out what those things meant.

She was also mindful of El Jefe's unseen presence that strongly discouraged men from taking an interest in her. Fortunately, she had some reasons for coming to the hacienda that she hoped would conceal her real intentions—such as visiting La Señora; picking up new Dream Wrecks for her gallery; or, as it worked out later, posing for the family portrait.

El Jefe, she told Mitch, wanted to pick the right man for her at the right time. But she decided to let Mitch know *he* was the right man. She decided to work as hard as she ever did to promote and market his Dream Wrecks—hoping her all-out effort on his behalf would communicate her growing attraction to him. She smiled at that point. "Could you tell I was coming on to you—in my own way?"

Mitch told of the thrill of her visits to his studio. At the first meeting, she seemed unobtainable: so poised, so sophisticated, and so beautifully dressed. And to top it off, a magical laugh and a luscious smile. With each visit, however, he felt less distance between them. Her supercharged promotion of his works was an example of her doing something for him above what would normally be expected. He knew she had invested a lot of time, money, and creativity on his behalf. He knew that kind of goodness was not something a distant or unreachable person would do.

On an earthier note, he noticed her body seemed to be more conspicuously clothed with the passing weeks—terrain only discreetly traveled with his eyes.

The humanness beneath her sophistication put him at ease, and he became confident he could, if not fascinate, at least interest her. She chuckled, a little embarrassed at that, but Mitch went on to say he imagined that, like painting the ocean or the high plateau, his imagination explored what her geography and light caramel skin would look like—when it was all there to see. Her face reddened, and she breathed deeply.

"Oh Mitch, you devilish artist—free to imagine every-thing and outrageous enough to blurt it all out—to someone you have only hugged before."

"Couldn't help it—had to tell the truth."

"My thoughts about you, *muchacho*, were not so *picante*."

"Now don't hold out on me, Amparo." Mitch's grin sneaked out. "What kind of salacious thoughts were you having?"

"Yes, I thought about you, but in a more restrained way," she said, as she put her hand on his. "How you would hold me and kiss me…how we would spend hours together, just talking and drinking wine, like we are right now. And how I could take a break from my hectic life and just be with you, watching you at work, painting and hearing your crazy jokes."

"That's a good beginning, Mi Amor."

Raindrops were starting to fall as they left the little restaurant and walked the dark streets back to their hotel. They playfully argued about whose suite to go to and decided not to go to his with its artist gear everywhere but to go to hers—fresh and clean as it was—for their new beginning.

Thunder, lightning, and torrential rain composed the music for their first night of love. The next day's constant drumming of rain was needed to catalyze the hours of serious and nostalgic remembrances they had to reveal—and talk through. From the hotel's tiny kitchen, they found straightforward Mexican dishes perfect for a rainy day. Mitch laughed off the drenching as he ran through the rain to bring food up to their suite, fueling the nonstop recounting of their life stories.

Their conversation was interrupted by surges of erotic energy that couldn't be restrained, even if they wanted to.

Then the conversation resumed. Amparo had to know if Mitch was ever married or had any children and what his family was like. His family was smaller than hers, and his mother was his star—the one who shone above the scattering of aunts, uncles, and cousins that lived in the Midwest. His mom had passed away soon after he returned home from war. That was real tough.

Mitch knew what some of Amparo's family was like. He really liked La Señora but wasn't sure he wanted to meet any more of her relatives. He had to know how much Amparo knew about El Jefe's drug business. She said not much—as the rich, powerful uncles were intensely secretive and told everyone they worked in the import/export industry and had a well-known, legitimate company. Aside from a loan to get her gallery started, she had no financial dealings with them.

Of course she had heard stories of narcotics trafficking and avoided believing them. She admitted she was probably in denial. Maybe she couldn't face the consequences of rejecting the protection of a person of great power—or facing his disapproval if she rebelled against his influence.

Mitch told her of his parents' divorce; how he was happy living with his mom, even during his Art Center years; and his rash decision to join the marines. He wanted to show that artists could be tough and shipped off to Iraq and Afghanistan. His girlfriend left after his return home—when the war's hangover drove him to the depths of anger and despair. His girlfriend was OK, he told Amparo. It was his craziness that drove her away.

Was she torn up with Uncle Max gone? She replied that she was saddened when she thought of younger days when his presence filled her father's place after his death. In her teenage years, Tio Max was very strict about boys—but that is not unusual in Mexico.

As an adult, his strictness made itself subtly known, and young men of her *milieu* were friends—but never came close. She resented that but knew someday she would find her own guy and lead her own life. This mild resentment turned to full-on hatred when she found out he planned to kill Mitch. But she felt a little bit bad about hating him so much, now that he was dead.

Mitch explained his art-therapy stages and talked of Burt, his shrink, who found a way for him to head back to normalcy. He talked of the special days along the coast with Chad and Surfer and other artist friends. He told of good times, lots of laughs at Malibu Seafood after painting, and his development as a painter, leading up to painting Fidel in an hour—and his kidnapping.

"I am committed to making it as an artist," he said. "I need it to stay sane, and I think I have the talent to make a living at it."

———

The following day, brilliant sunshine sent storm clouds packing up and moving out. The lovers walked along San Miguel's narrow sidewalks to a café filled with tourists about to take the Sunday home tour. Sitting at a remote table, they were already practicing their furtive life, existing in corners, in shadows, in out-of-the-way places. To be unseen faces in the crowd suited them. Particularly now when each other provided all the company they wanted.

The conversation changed course: What to do next?

"Checked online. I need a passport to get back into the United States. No way am I going to the American consulate because they would report to the US government that I am down here. Also, I'm here in Mexico illegally," he said. "Never did come in the front door.

"But I have a plan, Amparo—a plan that keeps me close to you for the next six months."

"Only six months, Mi Amor?"

"Right now it is too overwhelming to look very far ahead."

Touching his hand softly, as she often did to make a special connection, and looking intently in his eyes, she said, "Tell me your plan, Mi Amor."

"I will stay in Mexico for six months painting the Sierra Gorda..."

"Why there?"

"I am excited about painting the high, empty plateau of Central Mexico. I need that fix, like painting the ocean. Also been checking out the Sierra Gorda area online—it goes from the high plateau to incredibly rugged, high mountains and deep valleys. Interesting area and I think neglected by other artists.

"And we'll see each other on weekends. Either I take a bus to Mexico City, or you come out to see me as I wander around the towns there."

She said, "That's not too far for me."

"This way I build a body of work to sell. I live quietly, taking precautions not to attract attention that might tell Fidel or the government where I am. I won't stay in the same place very long. We communicate by e-mail from Internet cafés, using fake e-mail drops where we read and write draft messages that we don't send. No more telephone calls, too risky."

"And after six months?" she asked, with a little frown forming.

"We get married after the Pensamientos Febriles III exhibition in Los Angeles."

"*Que bueno,* Mitch!" She clapped her hands together. "It's all I could ask for—you forever."

Mitch said, "For the next six months, the weekends will be heaven."

She replied, "But the days apart, I'm afraid, will be filled with longing."

"I know, mi Amor, but that's when I turn my burning desire into new and intense art. That's how I am going to make a living and provide for us."

She said, "That's when I apply my love's energy to planning for the LA exhibition and building the mystery of the reclusive Ricardo."

Mitch frowned and said, "You know, Amparo. I don't feel real comfortable being described as a recluse, now that I am free."

Amparo took his hand and looked into his eyes. "If we reveal who you are, then you must go home to LA to avoid threats to your freedom and your life."

"Couldn't do that, Mi Amor. I can't live up there so far away from you."

Amparo brightened and said, "You were a recluse at first because you were a prisoner of Tio Max. Now you are a recluse because you are building a life's work with your art and building a future for us. Neither of these are dishonorable, Mi Amor."

"Looking at it that way, you are right, Amparo. But when I go home for the big exhibition in LA, we will let everyone know that Ricardo Casa DeSpiritu is really Mitch Alexander."

"Of course, Mitch, then there is no reason to continue under your nom de art."

———

After five days, their interlude was over, and Amparo went back to Mexico City. Mitch lived quietly at the Posada Ermita for close to another month. Amparo visited him another couple of times. In between her visits, he traveled in the countryside with car and driver from San Miguel Tours to paint the great expanses and to sight-see in neighboring towns. And then it was time to move on—toward the Sierra Gorda region.

With everything, except his easel and a few canvases in various states of completion, packed into his two new suitcases, he was ready for his next port of call—Querétaro.

His gray, cotton work duds and high-top work shoes gave him a more proletarian appearance than the blue denim and huaraches he wore back at the hacienda. With his hair growing longer and his beard coming in, he was starting to hide his facial features enough, he believed, that when topped off with his wide-brim straw hat and sunglasses, he would blend unrecognized into the crowd scene.

He was confident that anyone from the submarine or the hacienda passing him on the street wouldn't know who he was—except maybe, Fidel.

Chapter 36

QUERÉTARO

Santiago de Querétaro was beautiful in a way that all Mexican colonial cities are, with architecture evocative of splendor and tragedy. Its beauty was not evenly spread—like anywhere else. But there were many monuments and historic places that, taken all together, reflected a turbulent history of great cultures in conflict that produced modern Mexico.

Mitch took a taxi from San Miguel for the one-hour ride to Hotel Rincon de Querétaro. Driving into the city, he sensed the optimism of a place with industrial and cultural vitality. He had booked a reservation online, under the name of Greg Miller, and indicated his preference for a long-term stay and payment in cash.

Mitch was ready, if asked for ID at check-in, to claim that his pocket was picked—and he would get new papers from the American Consulate the next day. Checking into his modest suite, however, was uneventful. The desk clerk did not ask for ID, and Mitch told her he planned to be there at least a month and paid seven thousand pesos for two weeks in advance. The ID anxiety was off his chest—for now.

Mitch stowed his belongings in his suite and set out on foot. He found an Internet café three blocks away. Sure enough, there was Amparo's e-mail draft waiting for him—and he eagerly read it—then printed it for reading again later.

There was much to write about, Mitch thought while typing his return message for her: leaving San Miguel after their time together, finding out so much about each other, asking new questions about her life, telling how his artwork is progressing, and expressing the love and his longing for her that always ended his messages.

Mitch paid twenty pesos for his hour online and headed back to the hotel through the bustling evening crowds. He stopped at a Japanese restaurant for dinner and a couple of beers. He savored the anonymity of Querétaro—he knew no one—and no one knew him.

The next day Mitch walked for hours among the historical venues, taking in sights, eating in little cafés, and drawing sketches to give substance to his impressions. From an Internet café, he opened Amparo's new message, drinking in her words about preparations for the LA event and her love for him. He printed it for rereading back at the hotel—to lift up his spirits in the lonely evening hours. He left a long draft for her with details of his day and descriptions of his sight-seeing discoveries.

Mitch's messages to her were without reservation. Maybe it had to do with their reunion in San Miguel, where they spent days talking in a direct, honest way to release the pressure of months of restraint. He bared his soul—the good, the bad, the in-between—without searching for words better than the first ones he typed at the computer terminal.

Amparo took a bus to meet Mitch that weekend. They played at being carefree tourists, visiting the ancient aqueduct and lounging in sidewalk cafés long into the night. She was full of news of the outside world. But still no news of Fidel's whereabouts. Cousins she had coffee with said both Mexican and American security people were looking for him and had questioned some of their relatives. The idyll ended after two days when Amparo boarded the bus to Mexico City with her bag and a carton of his works.

Mitch found a travel agency, Sierratour. Their helpful guide, Rogelio, drove him to open spaces in the countryside and to sleepy villages where he could paint for a day, share a meal or two, practice Spanish, and then drive home with the setting sun. With a little scouting around they found panoramas made to order for putting an artist in the zone— especially if there was a breeze blowing or just bees buzzing. Nature's tonic came in different bottles, but it was all good for the soul.

———

Two weeks after Amparo's visit, with his beard still short, but trimmed and distinguished looking, Mitch took a bus to Mexico City. At their rendezvous, the Maria Cristina Hotel, the blend of guests was right for fitting in: European professionals and their bored wives meeting for a conference, tourists of various stripes, and singles and couples of ordinary people.

A detached building on the grassy lawn in front of the hotel housed a little bar where they sat in the dark corner. She was without makeup, hair in a simple bun, brim hat, sunglasses, and a homespun cotton jumpsuit.

"Mitch, an American couple came to my gallery yesterday. They asked if I was related to the late El Jefe. Maybe they were just curious when they noticed I had the same family name."

"Watch out, Mi Amor. Tell them nothing. Might be the Americans investigating drug cartels, or they might be looking for me. Did you sell them a painting?" he asked with inquisitive eyebrows and big grin.

"No, Señor *Comediante*, but I did sell them a catalog of the Berlin Pensamientos Febriles II exhibition for two hundred dollars."

"You sold a catalog for two hundred dollars! You are without shame—sin vergüenza, *bandita mia*."

"I am sin vergüenza," she whispered in his ear. "Let's go upstairs and make love before dinner."

Later, after showering and drying each other off, they dressed and walked to an old-world French restaurant a block away.

"You know, Mitch, you are doing well as an artist," she said, as she slipped him a packet of seventy-five thousand pesos under the table. "And there is a lot more in your account. The licensing of Ricardo Casa DeSpiritu is exploding. Besides tequila and T-shirts, you are about to be selling wine, luggage, automobile interiors, and golf bags."

"I can't believe I am in love with an angel—and getting rich too."

"I am número uno at this kind of promotion, but it would be nothing without the impact of your art. There is something that can't be described, that communicates with people right from your soul when they see your work. That's why they all want a piece of you and will pay for it."

The dinner tempo was slow, suiting their need to talk about their lives—mostly about their histories, but also about dreams, aspirations, things that made them laugh. The wandering violinist sensed good vibes and played "Estrellita" on the first pass by their table, and Amparo slid a little closer to Mitch, thighs touching. On the return pass, while the lovers whispered over coffee and brandy, the violinist reached for *romance máximo* with "Yours Is My Heart Alone," earning a generous tip for the warm spell his music cast.

Next day they had a late start but fit in an afternoon at the Palacio de Belles Artes. The monumental impressiveness of Mexico's art treasures left Mitch in awe. Afterward Amparo suggested strolling around the Zócalo to witness the spectacle of the city's heart. In that giant plaza, thousands of people of every description were buying, selling, laughing, dancing as Aztecs, moonwalking, begging, giving, and playing—in the shadow of the cathedral built in the time of the conquistadors.

Exhausted by their stroll, they went to the fifth-floor restaurant overlooking the Zocalo. Looking down from the balcony, they saw the Mexican flag lowered at sunset. Soldiers marched out of a barracks across the great plaza and formed two lines facing each other. A single file of twelve troops then marched out between them, carefully caught the biggest flag Mitch ever saw, as it came down to their waiting shoulders, and marched back into the barracks with it.

"There is so much more for me to see here," said Mitch, excited with his first two days in the city. "Looking forward to coming back."

"I hope we can," said Amparo, seeing the waiters lighting candles on the tables.

Mitch was busy buying a rose for her and didn't notice the tentative note in her voice. He refilled their wine glasses. They clinked and looked out again on to the Zocalo at dusk without saying anything. The moment was enough.

Back in the hotel Mitch used a guest computer in the lobby to e-mail Burt that he was OK. *Hard to trace my location here in a sea of twenty million people,* he thought, while logging on.

Addressed to Dr. Burt Philorubius, he wrote: "I'm OK Doc. Feeling great now and still painting a lot to keep my psyche on an even keel. Please DO NOT DIVULGE this message to anyone. I know I can trust you because of that doctor-patient-confidentiality business. And well—I just trust you. Up till now, I was afraid to get word out that I am alive. Even though I can e-mail now, having other people or the press know where I am could put me or my loved one in danger. Have much to tell you when I get back. If you see Chad, Surfer, or Kathy just tell them you *believe* I am alive. Nothing more. Very best, Mitch."

On their last morning together, Mitch and Amparo headed for the vast central bus station, where sleek silver buses fan out to all parts of the country. They got to the Querétaro bus with ten minutes to kill before its 11:00 a.m. departure.

Amparo surprised him when she said it was too risky for him to come to Mexico City again. She couldn't totally relax for fear of someone recognizing her with him. "Mi Amor, I just know too many people here that I could run into. And I have a bad feeling that the gringo couple's interest in me isn't going to end with a few questions. I will come to where you are on weekends. I will make it impossible for anyone to follow me."

"Not fair to you," said Mitch, "making the trip every time."

"*No es problema*," she said lightheartedly.

"Besides, there is so much more I haven't seen here."

She took his hand and said, "We better wait for a while and let the memory of these couple days bring us back sometime in the future."

After an I-don't-care-who-sees-us kiss, he climbed on board. A pretty attendant gave him a box lunch for munching on during the Charles Bronson movie. He wasn't sure he would stay awake for the movie in that comfortable reclining seat—and he didn't. Love had taken its toll.

———

Amparo commuted to Querétaro by chauffeured car the next four weekends. She varied the pickup times and places to shake off possible followers and used the traveling time to catch up with paperwork. During these weekends with Mitch she managed to forget about business. The hours played softly on their hearts, with the biggest job during her visits being the decision of where to go for dinner.

The following weekend Amparo came to his Querétaro hotel in her Range Rover. They drove to see the Peña de Bernal Monolith, an hour's drive away. This massive rock, over eleven-hundred-feet high, jutted out of the earth like a jagged blade and towered over the village on the flatland to the southeast. They meandered through a couple of gift shops to the compact Plaza Principal at the end of the main street. She bought each of them Peña de Bernal T-shirts and a couple books about Bernal and the Sierra Gorda.

A mustard-yellow church with red trim stood at the far end of the plaza. The church and the immense monolith in view a mile away materialized on Mitch's pad in ink and watercolor.

"Mitch, you are taking me to places I have never seen before."

"Fun, ain't it?" He held up a sketch for her to see.

"You got a bit of all of it: palm trees, white benches, a few people not hurrying anywhere, old-fashioned lamp posts, church."

"Not to mention the monolith," Mitch said. "It rates right up there with Gibraltar and Sugar Loaf in Rio."

"Didn't know it was world-class," Amparo said, surprised.

"Your friends are obviously not rock climbers; they would know all about such things?" Mitch chided.

"I spend too much time with city folks," she admitted.

Mitch said, "It helps to leave those city folks behind and breathe some fresh air every now and then."

They drove back to Querétaro before dark.

That night they had a simple dinner at Taco Llama and lingered at their outside table afterward sipping beer.

She asked, "Do you know that you talk to yourself? And even in your sleep?"

Mitch, distracted by a different thought, said, "It's time for me to move on. Been here six weeks."

Amparo said, "I am relaxed and comfortable here. I don't mind you talking in your sleep either. Stay longer, Mi Amor."

"Can't get too comfortable."

"Where to next?" she asked, with a hint of irritation.

"Jalpan."

"Why Jalpan?" she asked with a frown. "It's out in nowhere—a long drive from Mexico City."

Mitch said, "I've read there is some unbelievable terrain in the Sierra Gorda Mountains to the east of Bernal. I'll be honest with you; I want to paint it."

"A long way for me to drive." Amparo frowned.

"A long way—that's true," said Mitch. "But we are just talking three or four weeks, Mi Amor."

With a soft punch to his arm, she said, "It's OK if it makes you happy. You wanted to capture the Sierra Gorda on your canvases. And you should, Mitch. Who knows if we ever come here again?"

"And if I keep moving, there's less chance of the bad guys catching up," said Mitch.

"OK, we've got two good reasons to go to Jalpan," she said, happy again.

Chapter 37

JOC ON THE TRAIL

It was two months after the raid on the hacienda. Commander Heartworthy and three of her JOC team were in conference. Homeland Security had reduced her budget and refocused her mission on finding residual criminal activities of the Terrasombra cartel in the United States. She asked the team what they knew about the remnants of El Jefe's cartel.

The CIA representative, Rex Smith, said, "Top and mid-level cartel members were pretty much rolled up and arrested by Mexican forces. Maximilliano's brother Fidel is still at large. We don't have anything on him, as he has no arrest record or extradition request from Mexico; we are not treating his capture as high priority."

Myron Wolf added, "We rounded up over twenty Mexican Nationals. They are being deported. Street-level gangbangers working for El Jefe's cartel are still out there. They weren't loyal to El Jefe's crew, as they were treated like day laborers. They aren't sad he's gone. Where we have hard evidence, we'll work with local police to make arrests."

The commander asked, "Rex, what is the status of our ground assets in Mexico?"

"Surfers were sprung from jail after we told Mexican Intel about the submarine cruising to Malibu. They have returned home and been reassigned. French Scientist got a job at the submarine dock and is now working for Mexican Intel with our blessings. Taco Vendor is still in Mexico, on leave visiting his folks but ready to go if we need him.

"Tourist Couple is in Mexico City watching the Terrasombra family and friends. They are looking for obvious money laundering and checking the family assets and their businesses—particularly anything with US or other foreign connections."

"Did they find anything?"

"Not so far, but they are checking out a recent development. In Mexico City they found an art gallery belonging to Amparo Terrasombra, the niece of Fidel, who we saw being painted by Mitch Alexander. She's riding high in Mexico City right now. Her gallery also handles Ricardo Casa DeSpiritu, whose paintings sell like hotcakes—as do his products."

"Dudley, I'd like you to work with Rex to see if there's a connection between Amparo and the Terrasombra cartel fortunes, including any that might be parked here in America."

Dudley replied, "Roger that, ma'am."

"Any news of the artist, Mitch Alexander, who caused all this ruckus in the first place?"

Myron answered, "We have checked in some depth but can't figure out where he is. We know he's a vet, honorably discharged after combat duty in Afghanistan, cracked up mentally, and was institutionalized—got out and lived on the edge in a Bohemian artist complex.

"Then Mitch Alexander got into art therapy at the beach with a Chad Willoughby, the founder of something called Plein Air Expression. His artist buddies say he was well recovered mentally when he disappeared in Malibu. As you know, he disappeared again when the Mexican Army raided El Jefe's hacienda; it's possible they took him with them and just let him go. They didn't have any reason to hold him. Checked in LA and Alexander hasn't returned to his studio. We have word out to US consulates in Mexico to keep their eye out for him."

Dudley added, "We were ready to welcome him home with a trip to the White House and a bunch of TV interviews. After all that money we spent on him trying to save his sorry ass, he could at least have called and told us he was OK."

The commander responded, "We know Mitch Alexander is a whack job. Uncle Sam wasted enough on him already, so let's focus our resources on checking out Amparo Terrasombra. She's our last chance to wipe out what's left of the cartel. Keep our Tourist Couple on her tail."

———

Two days later Commander Heartworthy and team were in the JOC with Galeria Amparo on a screen. A large red building with arched windows. Amparo had divided her gallery into a number of large rooms featuring different artists, working in various contemporary styles. A video of the interior displayed the rooms. There were ample framing areas and an office area on the second floor. Another screen displayed Tourist Couple, side by side, facing the teleconference screen.

Tourist Man reported, "We have checked out bank transfers with Mexican authorities and discovered that El Jefe loaned Amparo one hundred thousand dollars when she started her gallery six years ago. She paid it back with interest two years later. Her business today is very active and profitable, as Amparo has links with leading Mexico City interior designers and decorators.

"El Jefe's transactions with legitimate businesses were always visible and in accordance with normal banking practice."

Tourist Lady jumped in and said, "This is pretty typical, as the narcos want to substantiate their claims to be legitimate business people."

Tourist Man continued, "We have a camera on her business and the entrance of her high-security condo building. She works long hours every weekday, but on most weekends she disappears—using different means of transportation: sometimes by car, sometimes by bus, other times by plane, or even taxi. Don't know where she goes. We assume in Mexico because of the lengths of time involved. The secrecy of her traveling appears suspicious. A lot of money is flowing into her business lately. Don't know of any money laundering, but not discounting it at this point."

The commander said, "I want you to find out where she goes weekends. She may be consorting with people that are cartel related and trying to get back in play now that El Jefe is toast. Step up surveillance. The full resources of Homeland Security support you."

"Aye aye, ma'am."

"By the way," asked the commander, "what is the status of your spy gear?"

Tourist Man said, "We retrieved the drone a day after the raid, well away from the hacienda. Spider Bot walked home from the fight, and we picked it up a couple days later. Both are in the trunk of our car. Bird Bot was, as you know, killed in action."

Commander Heartworthy said, "I will send you a new Bird Bot of the latest design. You will be able to pick it up at the American Consulate in Mexico City next Thursday."

Tourist Man said, "Aye aye, ma'am." And the screen went blank.

Chapter 38

JALPAN

From service in Afghanistan, Mitch developed an awareness of danger and a sense for how to avoid it. He told Amparo to always be aware of people she saw more than once in a crowd—they could be watching her. He stressed the need to avoid repeated behaviors. They changed their secret e-mail account every week or so. On visits to be with him, she dressed in a plain, rustic style—devoid of the chic touches of her big-city look. She was hardly recognizable—as was he, with his beard and shaggy locks.

Mitch's routine was now practiced and easy. Living quietly in the Jalpan Rancho Hotel under the name of Greg Miller, he maintained a low profile. His searches on the hotel computer didn't unearth anything indicating he was of interest to the authorities. He felt pretty safe.

Back in Querétaro, Mitch had downloaded a California driver license in an upscale Internet café. He rented time on a Photoshop-equipped computer and put the name Greg Miller on it, printed it, and had it laminated to look authentic. He didn't drive with his fake license. It was OK for checking into hotels but not good enough to pass the scrutiny of cops who might stop him or soldiers at rural roadblocks. Odd how having an ID, even a bad one, made him feel more comfortable—as long as he was not driving.

When there was driving to be done, Mitch hired a local guide. The latest, Alberto, talked enough to break the quietness of his days out there in the country. Mitch enjoyed his company and a chance to learn more Spanish. Alberto drove him out to paint, to sight-see, and to get into town for personal needs or occasional restaurant meals. He never asked questions about areas of Mitch's recent past that would be awkward for Mitch to lie his way around.

Mitch avoided talking with Americans who occasionally stayed at the Rancho Jalpan because of their usual questions: Where you from? What do you do? Etc. He feared a slipup in answering could threaten his anonymity. Maybe he was a little paranoid, but better safe than sorry.

There was a price to pay for his self-woven cocoon of isolation—loneliness. He relied upon the imagination of Alberto to come up with places to explore that offered the chance to brush elbows with other human beings.

One day Alberto suggested they visit the Franciscan mission in Jalpan. The Franciscans, who would spearhead the Spanish colonization of California, began their mission building there two thousand miles southeast of San Diego—the southern terminus of their chain of California missions. The mission tour offered opportunities for small talk and a few questions of the Franciscan brother leading it. Bar Jalpan, a few blocks away from the mission, was another opportunity to schmooze—with Gordo, the jovial bartender.

Alberto had the right touch with Mitch—segueing into Spanish lessons when they ran out of things to say. Didn't get much painting done, but it was a good day, and Mitch had a lot to tell Amparo using their e-mail drop.

So it went, most days grinding out paintings. The occasional day thrown in for sight-seeing and a bit more human contact. The Sierra Gorda unfolded its secrets, and Mitch knew he made the right decision to paint its unexpected delights. He knew coming in that there would be lonely days along the way. Not a big price to pay for the rewards of painting the unexpected and the promise of fulfillment when Amparo would again appear.

———

When back in Mexico City, Amparo let the flushed feeling happen. She focused on building the gallery business and taking care of the endless details of international licensing deals. She took on the top LA intellectual-property lawyer, Gunnar Huegelmeyer. He ensured her many product deals were guided toward rapid completion—with ironclad contracts and maximum protection from counterfeiting and transaction fraud.

Because of the distance, Amparo commuted to Jalpan by flying to a nearby airport, renting a car, and driving to

Mitch's hotel. For the upcoming weekend, Amparo decided to vary her routine by driving her own car. Driving would also allow her to take back paintings stacking up in Mitch's room.

She left the parking space in her condo basement early Friday morning—with something she hadn't packed: a limpet transponder held on to her rear bumper by a powerful magnet.

Shortly thereafter, the SUV carrying the Tourist Couple pulled away from the curb onto a nearby street—and followed far enough back not to be noticed. Driving to Jalpan took seven hours with one stop for gas and a taco. Rugged, primordial shapes of the Sierra Gorda Mountains blew away any hint of boredom from the drive—and kept Amparo awake while cruising the empty, sun-drenched roads.

She began to understand Mitch's fascination with wide-open, wild nature. He told her how when he started painting the ocean it brought him out of the morass of despair. When she asked how, he told her there was no textbook answer. He would paint, forget the cares of life, and go into his zone. There he experienced joy. It just happened.

He believed there was a kind of vibration or earth force that could connect with his mind when he relaxed in the zone. It was a positive force that continued to soothe his mind hours after coming out of the zone. It brought normalcy back to his life. The visual impact of these violently shaped mountains excited Amparo's senses, she was beginning to feel what she thought Mitch experienced on the way into the zone.

———

Amparo was exhausted and yearning for a swim as she pulled into the Jalpan Rancho Hotel. She changed into a black bikini and joined Mitch at the pool to float in a weightless suspension, to whisper and laugh, to look into the soft blue sky and drink in the happiness of being together. After a leisurely swim they sat in the round, brick sweat lodge for as long as they could stand it. The cold plunge and vigorous half-hour massages by Magdalena in the little poolside hut left them tingling. Back by the pool they ordered cold beers, and talked quietly until sundown. When they left the only other person there was a lady wearing a wide-brim straw hat at the far end of the pool.

Mitch said, "Amparo, the Dream Wreck spring has dried up; I am not having nightmares anymore. But I do paint many mornings—something fast and abstract. Like keeping a journal, but I don't write down my morning thoughts—I paint them."

Amparo said, "I saw them out in the room when I changed—it's exciting work! The LA exhibition will reveal your progression from the Dream Wrecks, when you were captive, to these more upbeat works reflecting your freedom. The theme will be all about your recent works—still high energy but now with more color, complexity, humor, and nuance." She kissed him lightly. "Your fascinating humanness continues to reveal itself, Mi Amor."

Alberto was indispensable because he knew the way to mountain heights from which they could survey great expanses of jungle under towering clouds. Amparo again experienced the awe of nature observed intently that was the driving force of Mitch's sanity.

She watched him standing at his easel, painting with total concentration. He applied paint forcefully with definite, strong strokes—no wimpy scrubbing. After he applied a brush load of paint, he walked back a few paces to observe the result. Then another attack on the canvas in response to inner forces that he did not fully understand. An occasional comment between them and the break for lunch that Alberto packed were all that intervened into his painting process. A rhythmic process that transformed a blank canvas into a carpet of jungle between him and a horizon serrated with the surreal shapes of the Sierra Gorda.

Those halcyon hours came to an end in the afternoon with Mitch running out of creative gas. Amparo could have relaxed longer in the chaise lounge with her novel about an art forger, when he announced, "Pool time." Reluctantly she folded her chair and umbrella. He called to Alberto fishing in the stream below, "*Vamos,* Amigo."

On the way back, Mitch told Amparo that green was the hardest color to capture on canvas. The jungle was a real challenge. Mitch dug into his bag of artist tricks to keep his recent works from getting the dreaded "case of the greens" with its unpleasant, greenish cast on the whole canvas. Amparo appreciated the insights into the artist's craft. It was of never-ending interest to her, and on the business side, her ability to interest clients in her artist's works was strengthened by this kind of insider information.

A Mexican couple with three kids, swimming, jumping, running, yelling, and the lady from yesterday, with her face hidden under the big straw hat, were their only pool company. Back in their room, they showered together and then soaked in the bareness of their bodies as intently as Mitch had devoured the jungle's secrets at the easel that afternoon.

Love, room service, sleep, and the day was done. Done for everyone except a gold finch peering through their high, round window.

It flew back to another room in the hotel for a recharge after Mitch turned off the light.

Chapter 39

UP CLOSE

Commander Heartworthy and her team had been flashed a picture of Amparo and her lover swimming in the Rancho Jalpan pool. She said, "Here's a surprise for you all: we have found out where Amparo Terrasombra spends her weekends. I'm disappointed she didn't lead us to any industrial-strength trafficking or money laundering. But we are not giving up on that possibility yet.

"Amparo's lover is an artist—American, bohemian-looking, as you can see. Did a jungle painting that doesn't look like anything in her gallery. Don't know who he is yet. Not sure they are up to anything, but our people in Mexico have been told to keep a close tail on them."

Dudley Henshaw said, "Hope yuh didn't put your Surfers back in action."

"No, we have Tourist Couple on their trail," said the commander authoritatively. "After months of trying, they put a limpet transponder on Amparo's car and followed her to

Jalpan, a town of about ten thousand in Central Mexico. They are staying in the same hotel as Amparo and her lover."

Dudley asked, "Can Tourist Couple handle themselves in a shootout?"

"They are in better shape than they look," the commander said with a straight face. "As CIA agents, they have to maintain personal weapons proficiency."

Dudley again asked, "What are their surveillance orders?"

The commander replied, "Tourist Couple is to maintain surveillance of the targets whenever they leave the hotel. That way if Amparo makes contact with any bad guys, we'll know it. We are trying to determine if drug money flows through her business empire—and to or from whom it flows."

———

Unbeknownst to the commander, Tourist Couple, now both in the room of Tourist Man, used Bird Bot to watch Mitch and Amparo in their room two doors away. They did not activate the live feed back to the JOC—their orders were to surveil their targets when they were traveling outside of the hotel. Tourist Man felt it was important to watch what was going inside Mitch and Amparo's room to be ready to surveil them if they decided to leave.

On a laptop, Tourist Couple watched the lovers drying each other off after showering and applying skin lotion with massaging strokes to each other's entire body. Fortunately for Tourist Man, they left a light on for his full viewing pleasure.

Tourist Lady, not usually a fan of explicit sex, managed to warm up to the lovers two rooms away—as they explored each other's bodies in a playful and slow-paced manner. Watching Amparo massaging the lotion on Mitch, she said, "I think they are lovely, Don."

"Yes they are, Betty," he said and gave her a forceful kiss that was met with equal force.

Still watching the laptop, they took their professional relationship to a new level for the first time.

Chapter 40

FIDEL ON THE BEACH

Following his departure from San Miguel de Allende, Fidel rented a place at Playa Negra. In the secluded house on the beach, there was the solitude he needed—until the dark cloud over his spirit would blow away. A short walk from the house was a cantina that suited his need to drown memories of his brother's death.

His comfortable job as general-purpose troubleshooter for Maxi's cartel was a thing of the past—nothing left to troubleshoot. He thought about rebuilding Maxi's operation, but realized the difficulties: recruiting a crew; killing off the competition; and avoiding the government. He knew he was not the guy to take on that kind of risk. He wasn't driven to dominate a cartel like Maxi, who even as a kid had to be número uno.

When they were young, they didn't have much money. Now he had plenty of cash—enough for life. The big guys have insatiable drives for power and money. Fidel was realistic enough to know he didn't have the nature or the need for running a big drug operation. But he was driven with every ounce of his life force to take on something else—finding and killing the gringo artist. That was his mission.

He often looked back on that day in Malibu when Javier had the artist in his sights; he had only himself to blame for letting Mitch live. He always felt the artist was somehow hooked up with the cops. Had to be, to have the army arrive just hours before Maxi's guys were going to get rid of him.

Fidel checked news from Southern California regularly on the Internet. He knew that Mitch's return would be a big deal north of the border. If Mitch crossed the border, Border Patrol would have announced it to the media. Returning to Malibu or LA would have him all over the news, particularly with so much media coverage when he disappeared. Hadn't happened. He must still be in Mexico.

———

On this afternoon, almost three months after the death of Maxi, Fidel was on his patio. He slumped back into his bamboo chair and squinted toward the sun, slipping behind a ribbon of crimson, as it sank into the ocean. Draining his tequila, he thought, *I know I can find that hijo de puta.*

He remembered chatting with Panchito the afternoon before the raid. Panchito said the artista went to San Miguel a few of times to buy supplies. The artista told Panchito that part of Mexico, with its distant vistas, reminded him of the ocean, and he planned to paint it someday.

Pouring another shot, Fidel thought, *I know where to start looking. If he is in Mexico I'll find him. If he left, I'll follow him north and find him. In time, I will get him, make him whine for his life like a beaten dog, and then kill him.*

Earlier that day Fidel bought an old Camaro from a villager who needed fast cash. Its dull coat of gray primer paint was a good fit with his full beard and shaggy, long hair. When he pulled up at the cantina, one of the guys said he looked like a musician who needed a job.

Right then Fidel knew he was ready for the hunt.

That night he would celebrate with some fishermen he had gotten to know at the cantina—guys who laughed a lot, who didn't care how drunk he got, and who never asked questions.

Next day he would head for San Miguel de Allende.

Chapter 41

THE HUNT BEGINS

Fidel pulled the gray Camaro up to El Gato—Materiales Artisticos. Inside he was fascinated by the variety of paints, brushes, and equipment of all kinds. *Getting off track—damn hangover*, he thought. Shook his fog away when he saw the owner approaching to ask, "Can I help you?"

"I am looking for an artist who might be a customer of yours," said Fidel in a friendly voice. "He's a gringo—brown eyes, tall, in his thirties."

"Are you police?"

"No, nothing like that," Fidel said, with a chuckle. "I'm uh…a musician. This artist painted my portrait once, and now I have another job for him."

"We get a lot of gringos. When do you think he might have been here?"

"I know he came to San Miguel to buy supplies three to six months ago.."

The owner looked off, puzzled at first, but then brightened as a memory came to the fore. "Back about then a gringo came here a few times with two Mexicans. They bought a ton of oil paint and many canvases."

"That's him!" exclaimed Fidel. "Where is he now?"

"Hard to say. I do remember one thing that might help you: the last time I saw the artist he came alone, probably three or four months ago," the owner explained, rubbing his chin. "Same guy. I remembered he needed a shave. He was very excited about painting big panoramas out in the Sierra Gorda. I suggested he go to Querétaro and then head in the easterly direction to see some real open spaces and unusual mountain formations."

Pleased with what he heard, Fidel said, "Thank you. That's very helpful."

———

Fidel moved on to Querétaro. There he visited the art supply stores without any luck. No one was exactly sure they had or had not seen Mitch. He drove for days around the city, looking for artists painting outside. Didn't find many artists at the scenic points on his tourist map. The ones he found were usually at the aqueduct viewing spots and none looked like Mitch Alexander and none heard of him.

Fidel spent nights in bars, swilling beer and tequila to assuage the feeling of emptiness that came with living outside the cartel world that had been the source of his power and self esteem. He never wanted to get too attached to his girl-friends back in Morelia. He preferred the bachelor life and the temporary attentions of ladies along the routes that assignments from Maxi took him. Now in Querétaro, he relied on his ability to roll into a new city and make friends quickly on the shady side of town to once again dispel the gloom of his evenings.

Fidel's days were short: he got out of bed around noon; downed a few shots of tequila; left the out-of-the way hotel; ate breakfast, usually eggs or *menudo*—a favorite hangover cure made from tripe; and searched another day for clues to where the gringo artist might be.

After three weeks of searching without luck, Fidel was sitting at an outside table at Taco Llama, and said to himself, *What would a gringo, who doesn't speak much Spanish and who might not have a car, do to get out into the Sierra Gorda to paint? He could take taxis back and forth, but that was pretty unlikely. Could rent a car, but he didn't have a license, because we had taken it when we grabbed him. He could work with a travel service. Hmm…*

Time for some online investigating, he thought. Googling questions about traveling in and around Querétaro, he found tourist businesses with vans that took day or overnight tours into the Sierra Gorda. Might be something there.

After a few stops the next morning, Fidel struck pay dirt at Sierratours. In its tiny office, the owner told of a gringo answering Mitch's description. They had driven him around four or five days a week—usually to landscape painting locations and back.

The owner said, "Before leaving here, he showed me a painting of the great monolith, Peña de Bernal. That guy knows how to paint. Loves painting in the Sierra Gorda region, which starts there at Bernal—said he plans to spend several months there."

"Do you know how I can contact him?" asked Fidel.

"I think I can put you on the right track. You see, when it was time for him to leave Querétaro, our employee drove him to Jalpan and put him in touch with a friend of mine, Jesus Garcia. Jesus has a tour company called Viajes de Jalpan. That was within the last month."

"Thank you, you have been a big help."

"*De nada,* Señor, where you are going there aren't many people. You should have no trouble finding your artist."

A new determination appeared in Fidel's eyes as he slid behind the wheel of the gray Camaro.

Chapter 42

THE GARDEN OF JAMES

The morning after the magical day painting high in the jungle mountains, Mitch and Amparo decided to take a day off to visit Las Pozas. Edward James, an eccentric Englishman, built this fantasy garden in the jungle starting in the 1950s. Called the Garden of James by the locals ever since, it had been set in a mountainside of lush vegetation, with cascading streams and pools stepped along its sloping terrain. Throughout the garden Edward James built fantastic structures made of reinforced concrete in surreal deco shapes, upon which exquisite orchids and a profusion of vines found welcoming haven. Many trails wound through the garden site with connecting steps, ramps, bridges, and narrow, winding walkways traversing its eight hundred acres. Pathways wandered from marvel to marvel, under arched trellises and amid platforms, towers, and staircases jutting up to four stories.

The lovers drove to the garden in Amparo's Range Rover arriving about ten o'clock. There was just one other car in the parking lot. Never was much traffic in this isolated garden, so far off the beaten tourist paths. Today was no exception, the only other patron being a local priest, who had just walked in for a stroll during his morning meditation. Mitch and Amparo paid twenty pesos at the entrance and began exploring the quiet pathways. He was looking for a good spot for a watercolor sketch, and she was looking for dramatic photo opportunities.

Ten minutes later the SUV with Tourist Couple drove up. Tourist Man carried an oversized camera case and, under his shirttail, a pistol. Tourist Lady had a pistol under the front of a floppy blouse. In a remote spot in the garden, Tourist Man checked to make sure there was no one around. He took Bird Bot from his camera case and launched it with a flick of the wrist toward the blue sky. He guided it with his iPad as it climbed above the treetops, where JOC took control, sending Bird Bot to watch Mitch and Amparo. JOC stayed in contact with Tourist Couple through their hearing aid radios.

———

At the Jalpan Rancho Hotel, the desk clerk noticed a gray Camaro pull into a check-in parking space. The Camaro was dirty and in need of a new muffler—just like the driver who steamed right up to the front desk in a cloud of tequila and menudo breath. He loudly asked for the room number of the gringo artist staying there. The clerk maintained his cool and explained he wasn't allowed to give out room numbers.

Fidel, with a steely, locked-on stare, said, "I am meeting him here today."

To which the clerk, glad to give Fidel's menacing presence a reason to leave, said, "The artist is not here at the moment. He is visiting the Garden of James."

"Where is that?" asked Fidel gruffly.

"Keep going up the road for sixty-four kilometers. You will see a sign for Las Pozas. That's it."

About to leave, Fidel hesitated and asked, "Is the artist at the garden with anyone else?"

The clerk said, "He and Señorita Terrasombra have driven there together."

Fidel felt a physical jolt, looked at the clerk blankly, mumbled, "Gracias," and stamped out to his car.

Fortified with alcohol and hatred, Fidel was hell-bent on killing the gringo—now he knew just where to find him. The thought of Amparo with him—after all Maxi did for her— had his blood boiling. He obsessed on confronting Mitch and Amparo. *I'll kill him in front of her and let her live with that. Someday I'll kill her too.*

Driving maniacally to the garden, he skidded the Camaro into the parking lot. He jumped out of the car and pounded through the gate, ignoring a request for ten pesos. Like a madman on the hunt, he strode fast through a maze of walkways and paths—frantically looking right and left for Mitch. Sweat popped out on his forehead, Fidel began to jog through the humid jungle passages, muttering, "Fuckin' gringo, you're dead."

Rounding a blind turn covered with hanging orchids, he collided with Mitch, who was standing there painting a watercolor! They bounced apart. The memories of the Malibu portrait burned through the camouflage of long hair and full beards—they instantly recognized each other. Their pumps of primeval hormones pounded attack signals into their brains.

"Shit!" yelled Mitch, eyes wide with fear and hatred.

"You want shit? You get it," snarled Fidel, through curled lips—reaching for the pistol in his waistband. Mitch, with nowhere to retreat, punched him in the face with everything he had. Fidel staggered backward and fell to the path. His gun went off when his head clunked hard on the flagstones—and he let it go. Mitch jumped to the gun, picked it up, and aimed at Fidel who was slowly trying to rise.

Mitch's gun hand froze, as a flashback from Afghanistan suddenly faced him—forcing to memory the expression on a young *mujahidin's* face as Mitch shot him dead. *Can't kill again like that.*

"Can't do it." He gasped.

He couldn't shoot Fidel, but knew he had to stop him. Mitch did the next best thing: Holding the barrel, he slammed Fidel's face and head over and over with the butt of the gun. Fidel's attempt to get on his feet dissolved under the pounding. He began sinking down again to the stones.

Amparo had been wading in a pond to get a good picture of a cascading waterfall, when she heard shouts and a shot. She ran to where Mitch had been painting and saw him pummeling a man, who was slumping to the ground. She was horrified; her heart thumped hard seeing Mitch smashing a gun against the man's head.

"*Dios mio.* Stop hitting him!" Amparo screamed. Mitch stopped, ejected the clip from the gun and threw it into the dense vegetation, and then flung the gun in the opposite direction.

Violently shaking from shots of adrenaline straight to his heart, Mitch caught his breath and managed to say, "It's Fidel, just tried to shoot me."

"Ai yai yai," burst out of her mouth. She backed up a couple of steps, struggled to clear her brain, and tried to make sense of what was in front of her. "Mi Amor, we have to get you out of here. I'll pull the car up to the entrance. You wash the blood off yourself and get out there pronto." And she ran off.

He walked to a little pond and ripped off his blood-sprayed shirt. He rinsed his hands and face; dried them on a clean part of the shirt; threw it away—leaving him in a T-shirt; and walked fast toward the exit.

The trails were curved and complicated; Mitch figured he was heading the right way based on where the sun was—going east. Began running to get out of the garden before Fidel came to. It was taking longer than expected. Rounded a corner—and crashed into a bloody Fidel, now holding a revolver!

A jolt of terror gripped him, forcing out a loud, "Jesus Christ." Mitch jumped onto a circular staircase to evade Fidel's line of sight and raced upward. He headed up the winding helix with Fidel laughing and taunting, "You need

Jesus Christ. These stairs go nowhere." Mitch went higher and realized what Fidel meant.

Another of Edward James's puzzling monuments: twin circular staircases that went up forty feet and stopped. Amazing for the admirer of avant-garde structures—disaster for a man fleeing for his life. Fidel started up in pursuit, taking measured steps to avoid a fall from stairs with no handrail. With gun in right hand and left hand on the center column for support, Fidel plodded up the stairs.

Tourist Couple came running up. In communication with the JOC, they knew the situation Bird Bot was witnessing. Tourist Lady climbed the staircase behind Fidel. She had her gun out, and as Fidel got high enough to take a clear shot at Mitch, she fired. Just missed Fidel's head, spraying concrete dust into the air. Startled, Fidel turned and saw her. He shot right back at her, hitting her right leg. She slumped to the stairs. Managing to hold her gun toward the enemy as trained, she fired back, hitting Fidel in the left buttock.

Fidel knew he was hit. Undeterred, he took aim at Mitch when a shot rang out—this time fired by Tourist Man, from halfway up the parallel staircase. Reacting to the searing pain in his right shoulder, Fidel dropped his gun arm, and anguish spread across his face—his chance for revenge lost. Unsteady now Fidel lost balance, stumbled, and fell twenty feet to the ground—there writhing and groaning in agony.

Mitch descended the staircase and shouted, "Thanks, whoever you are," to the Tourist Couple, then ran to meet Amparo. Tourist Man helped his partner down the stairs. They headed for the gate as fast as they could. Tourist Lady was limping painfully. On the way out, they told the two wide-eyed attendants to call the Red Cross, because a man had fallen from the spiral staircases.

———

The priest, hearing the shots, broke off his meditation. He ran to the staircases shouting, "Stop shooting! Stop shooting!" He saw the Tourist Couple making their way out and a groaning Fidel on the ground.

With tears of pain and frustration flowing from his eyes, Fidel looked up at the priest and uttered through clenched teeth, "I want to kill that hijo de puta."

To which the priest exclaimed loudly, "Foreswear vengeance to save your soul from hell's fires."

"Sí, Padre, but that *bastardo* killed my brother."

"No matter, my son. You can't die with hatred in your soul. Do you want to confess your sins while you are still conscious?"

"Sí, Padre."

The priest leaned in closely, and they whispered through the steps of Fidel's confession.

Chapter 43

RINGSIDE

The commander was in communication with Tourist Man when he released Bird Bot in the Garden of James. He then turned its control over to a JOC controller via satellite link. After taking control, the JOC controller flew it above the tree-tops to survey the whole scene in the garden, while displaying its images on the main JOC screen. From above, the JOC team knew the locations of the five people in the garden. They saw Amparo's boyfriend painting a watercolor image of a ten-foot tall concrete flower and Amparo, camera in hand, shooting a waterfall from its pool below. They saw Tourist Couple tailing Amparo and her boyfriend unobtrusively. A man, who looked like a clergyman, was also strolling around.

The sound of screeching tires attracted Bird Bot's attention. The JOC team saw a gray Camaro careen into the parking lot and skid to a stop. A man with black, shaggy hair and unkempt beard jumped out, took a long pull on a bottle, and ran into the garden.

At that point the commander ordered, "Bring Bird Bot closer to Amparo and her boyfriend. This could be trouble." When the fight broke out, the controller lowered Bird Bot close enough to capture the action.

The JOC team came to life, with all eyes glued to the big screen. Everyone watched grimly as Amparo's boyfriend pistol-whipped his assailant. Everyone was pumped and excited as they saw the boyfriend start his getaway. But then the group groaned when he ran into a recovered assailant now with a revolver and was backed up on the stairway to nowhere. Wild cheers erupted as Tourist Couple came to the rescue, with the murderous assailant wounded by their shots and tumbling to earth.

Commander Heartworthy ordered the team to concentrate on the identification of the assailant in the garden. Might be some connection to the narco world. She then ordered the controller to get the Bird Bot in close enough to listen to the assailant's words to the clergyman kneeling over him. The commander thought these might be his last words, and they might have useful information for the war on drugs—and Amparo's possible involvement in it. In whispered Spanish and difficult to hear, the conversation was recorded for enhancement by information technology specialists.

———

An hour later, Tourist Man came up on a screen in a grainy Skype picture. He said, "Commander Heartworthy, I am sure you have witnessed the fire fight. We are in our hotel. I have disinfected and bandaged Betty's leg wound with my first-aid supplies. The bullet went through and through; no bones broken, and there is no more bleeding. Can't risk going to a hospital with a gunshot wound. That would draw in the authorities. We are withdrawing from Jalpan the way we came, and will await your decision for extracting us."

Commander Heartworthy responded, "Proceed as described Don and standby for further extraction orders. Let me congratulate you and Betty for a job well done.

"You two following Amparo Terrasombra as carefully as you have has borne real fruit."

Don, puzzled, looked over at Betty who was lying down with throbbing leg elevated. "What kind of fruit?"

"We ran a check on Amparo's boyfriend using your Bird Bot evidence from the hotel in Jalpan. Our analysts identified him as Mitch Alexander, Malibu's missing artist."

"Damn! We didn't recognize him the way he looked."

"That's not all. The other individual you may not have recognized was Fidel Terrasombra. The man you were shooting at. His long hair, beard, and pistol whipping made recognition difficult. We heard enough of Mitch Alexander and Amparo talking at the fight scene to convince us that he was indeed Fidel.

"He was taken in a Red Cross ambulance to Xilitla. He is in bad shape."

Chapter 44

TIME TO LEAVE

From the Garden of James, Mitch and Amparo sped back to the hotel. Mitch showered and changed at top speed. He put his recent paintings and suitcases in Amparo's Range Rover. Amparo was also rapidly packing and getting ready to walk out the door when Mitch's cell phone rang. *That's strange,* he thought. *Only Amparo knows the number.*

"Bueno…" he answered tentatively.

"Hello, Mitch."

Mitch frowned and asked, "Who's this?"

"This is Commander Heartworthy, from Homeland Security."

"How do you know my number?" asked Match.

"A little bird told me," said the commander in a cheerful voice.

"That's real droll, Commander," said Mitch, getting mad. "I don't have time to joke around."

"See the little bird on your windowsill?" asked the commander.

"Yeah, I can see it."

"See if you can catch it," she said.

Mitch walked quietly toward Bird Bot and made a grab for it, but it flew backward and hovered like a humming-bird just out of reach. Mitch thumbed his nose at the bird, which popped up immediately on the big screen at the JOC—getting a round of laughter from the commander's team.

"OK, Commander, what do you want?" asked Mitch, knowing he couldn't hide.

The commander said in a sympathetic tone, "Mitch, it is time to come home."

"Says who?"

"Our CIA people were on the scene today, and they saved your ass."

Mitch knew it was not the time for a flippant com-ment. "Saved more than my ass. Saved my life. I appreciate that and am indebted to you guys. But look, Commander Heartworthy; I am happy here. I am working at what I love and seeing the person I love—as your frigging little bird is telling you."

"We may not be there the next time to save you," said the commander.

"I'll take my chances."

"Be advised you have other problems," said the commander.

Mitch knew Commander Heartworthy was starting to make sense and beckoned to Amparo to listen in. He switched to speakerphone. "What kind of problems?"

"Number one, you are in Mexico illegally—no tourist card, no passport, no legal identification, and beyond the tourist time limit.

"Number two, Fidel, if he lives, will be out to get you again, and there might be other El Jefe fans that feel the same way he does.

"Number three, your disappearance from the Mexican Army raid has raised eyebrows about things no one wants to look into."

"Yeah, OK," said Mitch. "They are all my problems. Why are you so eager to fix them?"

"Our mission is to find an American citizen who was kidnapped. That's what we owe the public. We want to bring you back where you are safe. You have an obligation, Mitch, to those who love you and miss you to come back and at least let them know you are alive.

"After you come back, you can work on returning to Mexico legally, instead of living like a fugitive."

After a long pause in the conversation, Mitch returned to the line. "Commander, you've got some good points. Don't think we can handle many more days like today. I'll talk it over with Amparo—can you call again tomorrow?"

"Affirmative, let's shoot for four p.m."

"Roger that."

———

Mitch and Amparo rapidly finished packing their clothes and loading their suitcases in the car, along with Mitch's recent paintings. Mitch checked out of the Jalpan Rancho as nonchalantly as possible. He didn't want it to be obvious, but he was thinking they had to get the hell out of town before the police, army, or narco-thugs caught up with them.

A minute after paying the bill they were back on the road heading for San Miguel. There was an army checkpoint the other side of Pinal de Amoles, and Mitch was concerned he might not get through.

On the way into Jalpan, Mitch was with the Sierratour driver who was known at the checkpoint and got through with no problem. On the way out, in a car that was at the garden shoot out, it could be a different story. There might be an alert out for them. This thought knotted up his stomach for the two hours it took to drive there.

With Amparo at the wheel, they got waved through without a hitch. He thought, *Damn, I'm getting paranoid—maybe it really is time to go home.*

"Amparo, Commander Heartworthy had a point. I'm living every day looking over my shoulder. Afraid of the police. Afraid of Fidel. Next I'll be afraid of my shadow."

Amparo answered, "Mi Amor, after today they will get worse—your fears—I'm afraid."

"Amparo, here in Mexico I know I'll see you every weekend. Back in LA it will be six weeks before the exhibition. God, I hate the thought of not seeing you very often."

"Mitch, it is time for you to go home. I have to travel to LA to make arrangements…"

"How often will you be in town?" he asked.

"It won't be every week, but I have to be there a third to a half of the time to make sure everything is going OK."

Mitch said, "Gonna really miss you."

"But, Mi Amor, I'll be seeing you more in LA then here."

"I'm not going, Amparo," said Mitch. "I've gotten used to feeling good, feeling hopeful here in Mexico. That could change."

"You want to have our first fight, Gringo?" asked Amparo, with a hint of firmness in her smile, as she punched him in the thigh.

"Jesus you are tough."

They pulled into the Hotel Sierra after dark and got the room they had phoned ahead for. It was four and a half months since their first night in San Miguel. Dinner at the little restaurant of their first date was a tender touch to a mind blowing and exhausting day.

———

Up late the next morning, they wandered around town, checking out galleries and soaking up San Miguel's incredible sights. At four the phone rang.

"Hello, Commander Heartworthy," said Mitch.

"Thought things over, Mitch?"

"Yes, I am ready to go back to California," he said in a resigned tone.

"That's good news, Mitch. Looks like you are located in San Miguel de Allende."

"You got it," he said. "We're in a hotel in the middle of town."

"We'll have a plane at Leon International Airport tomorrow at three p.m.," said Commander Heartworthy.

"OK I'll take a cab there, but I don't have any ID."

"Forget the cab," said the commander. "We will pick you up from the Hotel Sierra at one p.m. You'll be traveling as a diplomatic employee, and we'll have a set of papers for you."

"Commander Heartworthy, I am a neurotically private guy. I don't want any publicity when I get there. Besides my mental problems, there are narco assholes out there that want a piece of me, and I don't want them to know I am back in LA."

"Don't worry; your safety comes first. Any press coverage will be minimal."

Mitch put down the phone and turned to Amparo. "It's done, Amparo. I'll be gone tomorrow. It's depressing me already."

Amparo said, "It's not easy for either of us, so here's what we are going to do tonight: we're booked for massages, facials, and haircuts in the spa in twenty minutes."

"You are an angel with a big heart, but I still don't want to leave."

"After the spa we'll have a candlelight dinner at La Capilla."

"Come on, Amparo! Now I really don't want to leave!"

"I'll be flying up to LA a few times until the big exhibition in six weeks. After that we're together forever."

A big grin and Mitch said, "I can do it."

While they walked the cobblestone streets to La Capilla, Mitch saw a headline on a vendor's stack of newspapers: "Fidel Terrasombra Survives Fall." He bought the paper to read the article: "Brother of notorious drug lord El Jefe, Fidel Terrasombra was seriously injured in a strange incident at Las Pozas, the Garden of Edward James in Xilitla. Falling eight meters from a helical stairway sculpture, he was unconscious when the Red Cross arrived on the scene. After regaining consciousness, he claimed that his two bullet wounds, one in the arm and one in the left buttock, were from shots fired by a tourist couple, possibly Americans. The couple and a Catholic priest, who gave him last rites after his fall, could not be found for comment. Señor Terrasombra is recuperating at the Xilitla Red Cross clinic. Authorities said he is in police custody and will be transported to a prison hospital in several days when his condition stabilizes."

After reading it together, they looked at each other and smiled. "Hot dog! Didn't mention us," said Mitch.

Amparo said, "We can relax and enjoy our last night together."

La Capilla again cast its magic spell as dusk turned to starry night. With the softest breeze causing their candle to flicker, they discussed plans for the LA event.

Mitch had an inventory of Dream Wrecks at the Brewery that Amparo wanted to see and draw upon, as needed, to fill the large gallery space at the Los Angeles County Museum of Art. Additionally, Amparo was accumulating new Sierra Gorda works in her gallery. She was going to introduce a few of them to titillate the followers of Ricardo Casa DeSpiritu with the promise of his work heading in a new, unexpected direction.

Amparo planned to hang one hundred works for Pensamientos Febriles III. They planned how they would split the work, with Mitch handling the paintings to be framed in LA and Amparo handling framing and shipping from Mexico City. She would also have an experienced team in LA producing the exhibition.

This last night in Mexico for Mitch was too full of memory and emotion for a lot of talk about business. Both knew that this time in Mexico that was now ending could never be repeated. Its mix of new love, danger, desire, surprises, fear, and happiness was finished.

Mitch had bought a gold necklace with two birds entwined at the famous Galeria Atenae that afternoon. He gave it to her as their evening out was drawing to a close—told her it represented them traveling together to wherever destiny leads them. Her eyes welled up for a minute as she put it on.

But then she got her smile out and put her hand on his wrist. "My present for you is a little more practical. I've opened up a bank account in Los Angeles with your earnings to date from our partnership. Put this checkbook in your pocket."

He took the checkbook, with a peek at its balance—raised his eyebrows. "That's a lot of dinero, *Amiga mia*."

"You earned every peso, Mi Amor."

"We're a good team."

"In many ways," she said with a wink.

Chapter 45

TOP SECRET

The day after the incident in the Garden of James, Fidel's confession was handed to the commander in a top-secret envelope. She had directed her IT specialist to produce a DVD of the Bird Bot feed with English subtitles and transcript. She had a hunch there would be something there that could be useful—but being privileged information, was not for public dissemination. She instructed that it be classified top secret with only one copy made—for her.

She told her administrator not to admit anyone for the next hour and then opened the envelope and put the DVD in her computer. She saw and listened to the priest, crouching over Fidel, who was lying face up in the dirt. The video and sound came through very clear, and she was impressed by the technology at her disposal.

English translation and subtitles on the DVD revealed this dialog:

"You have forsworn vengeance. That is good my son," the priest said. "Now let me hear your confession to put your soul in a state of grace."

"Bless me father for I have sinned. It's been thirty years since my last confession."

"Have you killed?" asked the priest.

"Sí, about twenty-five times. Pepito Morales was the first one I killed when I was eighteen. Then, to help my brother in the drug business, I mostly killed mayors, policemen, and gangbangers. I shot the governor of Baja, but he survived."

"You must do many good works to atone for this."

"Yes, I promise."

"Do you honor your parents?"

"Yes, I brought an artist from a great distance to paint Mamá's portrait."

"Bueno."

"Are you faithful to your wife?"

"Not married, Padre."

"Do you commit adultery or covet thy neighbor's wife?"

"Sí, Padre. I have a strong sex urge, but I try to stay away from married women."

"How many times have you committed sexual sins?"

After a pause, Fidel answered, "Probably four thousand times with women and slapping the monkey—maybe two thousand times."

"Cruelty to animals is something civilized people should avoid."

"Sí, Padre."

"If you live, my son, you should think of getting married to avoid sin and perversion."

"Sí, Padre."

"If God gives you a longer life, promise to reform and do good to atone for the great harm you have done."

"Sí, Padre."

The priest intoned Latin prayers of last rites and made a sign of the cross with his thumb on the forehead of Fidel, who was sliding into unconsciousness.

Commander Heartworthy slipped the DVD into its protective case and placed it in a hidden pocket of her briefcase. She thought, *We never had anything on Fidel—and now we have admissions of murder and cartel involvement. This could be huge.*

Chapter 46

DESTINATION LAX

Two serious-looking American men picked Mitch up at the Hotel Sierra. He said his good-byes to a tearful Amparo in the room. Out front one of the men put his bags into a black SUV. A tight embrace and meaningful kiss—then he was in the car with its darkened windows for the ride to the Leon airport.

Mitch's thoughts went back to Puerto Rana Verde where he first set foot in Mexico. Images cascaded through his mind of the extraordinary experiences that formed the last eight and a half months of his life.

For Mitch the high plateau and mountains of central Mexico had that same psychic stimulation as the ocean at Malibu—providing an unexpected lift to the grim wondering of where his kidnapping would lead, or how it would end. Now he was driving away with a touch of sadness. He left that thought—and brightened up with anticipation of seeing friends like Burt, Chad, Surfer, Kathy, and old familiar places—like Malibu Seafood.

At the airport Mitch flashed his new passport and tourist papers and followed the CIA agents to a white G-5. On board, he strapped in for takeoff and looked down during climb out, at the land that held part of his heart.

Flying away from Amparo shot off a shiver of fear that he might never see her again. He fought it by telling himself, *Cowboy up—our bond isn't one that will easily break.* Looking down at Mexico slipping away beneath the plane, Mitch tried to cheer himself up. *I gotta stop thinking like a prisoner or a fugitive. We can talk every day now. When she is in LA, we can walk in public with our heads held high.*

The plane leveled out at cruise altitude. One of the agents who picked him up at the hotel sat across from him. "Hi, Mitch, I'm with the CIA—name's Jeff Farley. I would like to start your debrief."

"Not wearing briefs, Jeff."

Jeff made a pained half grin—was not amused by the aged pun, "Mitch, you may have seen or heard things in Mexico that can help us with the war on drugs."

"I'm for that; what do you want to know?"

"Tell me where you were for the months since the raid on El Jefe's hacienda," said Farley.

"Basically I was leading the artist's life, living in modest hotels, painting out in the wide-open spaces from San Miguel de Allende to the Sierra Gorda and on to Xilitla. All the time I was hiding from Fidel and any other sympathizers of El Jefe."

"Why didn't you just come home?" asked Farley.

"I had personal reasons for wanting to stay in Mexico for a while. I didn't want to face a lot of attention from the press or police or government. I was panicked by that kind of stuff—still am. I didn't have close relatives or a wife that I would have an obligation to return to ASAP."

"How about Amparo Terrasombra? Did you have a personal or business relationship with her?"

"Now you are pissing me off, Jeff. This debriefing is over."

"Sorry, didn't mean to pry."

"Yeah, I know, just doing your job," Mitch said. Then he asked, "Got anything to eat or drink on this rendition rocket?"

Sandwiches and sodas were found and eaten without a lot of conversation thereafter. On the way to the toilet in the back of the plane, Mitch saw the Tourist Couple—Don snoozing and Betty awake with a bandaged leg up on the opposite seat. They made eye contact, and Mitch said, "Nice shooting. You guys saved my life. How can I thank you?"

"You just did. For government workers like us, saying thanks is just fine."

"Are you two married, by any chance?"

"No, but while working together as we have for months in Mexico, we have grown very fond of each other."

———

Leaving behind the views of the Mexican desert and Sea of Cortez, the G-5 entered US airspace and vectored to LAX. After landing, they taxied to a remote part of the airport, away from the commercial terminals. The door popped open, stairs extended. Mitch and the two CIA agents, who picked him up, descended first. Don and Betty followed—all to be greeted by an excited Commander Heartworthy.

"Welcome home, Mitch. I'm Jane Heartworthy, and I want to extend a warm welcome on behalf of a lot of happy Americans."

"Thanks, Commander Heartworthy."

"Mitch, there are a few members of the press here today. They are anxious to hear in your own words what happened to you since you disappeared while painting in Malibu."

"Goddamn it! Don't put me on TV or take pictures. I don't have anything to say now, except thanks to those who helped get me out of a tight spot in Mexico. When I get my brain and emotions under control, I'll have more to say. Where can I get a taxi?"

The commander ordered, "Jeff, give Mitch a ride home." And then speaking into the press microphones, said, "Mitch Alexander is back safe and sound. This is a great day for Homeland Security and all the unseen and unsung heroes that made his return a triumph of the American way.

"Mitch wants his privacy. We all understand that and will respect it. At this point we can't tell the whole story of his disappearance. As most of you have heard by now, he was kidnapped by a drug cartel run by the notorious El Jefe, who was killed several months ago in a Mexican Army raid.

"The day before yesterday, US agents, investigating the still-glowing embers of this cartel, discovered Mitch in a jungle location in Mexico. Our team intervened just in time to save him from death at the hands of Fidel Terrasombra, brother of El Jefe. At some appropriate time, we'll be divulging more information on circumstances of this case, but for now, we are all wishing Mitch a hearty welcome home!"

———

The CIA agents dropped Mitch off at the Brewery Lofts. Network news vans lurked there, waiting for him. He raced into the office to get a key to his place then double-timed it down the alley—ignoring reporters running alongside. Banging the door to his apartment shut behind him, he dropped his suitcases, looked around, and thought, *Jesus what a pigpen. After months of living in hotels I can really see how crappy this old pad is. Got to clean it or leave it. Not sure I want to stay here anyway, now that reporters and everyone else know where I live.*

An hour later reporters were gone, and he walked up to Barbara's café—getting a shriek from Kathy when he came through the door. Then a big hug.

"Mitch, you're back, and you are really looking good. How's your head?"

"I'm doin' good, Babe, pretty much back to normal."

"Were you really kidnapped?" asked Kathy, wide-eyed.

"Yeah."

"Thank God, you're safe. Where ya been?" Hoping for more details than he was willing to give.

"Mexico. When I get some time, I'll tell you about it," said Mitch. "Anybody here looking for me?"

"At first cops and FBI asking questions and searching your place. Of course, lots of reporters—just like today."

"Can I use your laptop for a minute?" Mitch asked.

"Sure you can, always could—you know that," she chided.

He wrote a draft in the secret e-mail account. "Mi Amor, just got back to the old digs. Sure looks crummy after living in some pretty decent hotels down there in Mexico. I'll be taking care of business the next few days. Will be getting my car out of impound, buying a phone, things like that—and contacting my friends and relatives.

"Now that I have a few more pesos, I'll move into a residence hotel like Oakwood Apartments. No one will know where it is but you. It will be our love nest during your trips to LA.

"Will still keep the Brewery loft and use it for a studio—and let the rest of the world, reporters, cops, CIA spooks, etc. think it is my real address. Funny, coming back from my life on the lam, I am finding it hard to unpack mentally. Keep thinking I am being hunted down. I hate the idea of so many people knowing where I live. That's why I don't want to stay overnight at the loft. Please bear with me until I mellow out. Besides, my Brewery loft just isn't love-nest certified."

"You, Mi Amor, are my morning star. Feeling sad and alone, but wildly in love. Mitch."

Chapter 47

IN THE NEWS

Commander Heartworthy threw a victory party to celebrate Mitch Alexander's return. She reserved a private room at Tooters in Manhattan Beach, and the JOC team let it all hang out. Tourist Lady linked in on FaceTime from her hospital room to greet everyone and got a hero's welcome for a brave accounting of herself under fire. The commander toasted her and shouted "Hurrah!" followed by a thunderclap of hurrahs!

Everyone made the scene but Mitch Alexander, who couldn't be reached by phone or courier. Nonetheless, the thoughts of all were with him. The partygoers were glad he made it back unharmed.

After two of hours of partying, Commander Heartworthy realized it was her duty to leave first. She left with a Jumborita glow still ascending and ordered her car brought up by the valet parking service. Before driving off, she opened the trunk to get the briefcase that held her Porsche driving glasses.

The briefcase was missing!

Knowing right away that she was in trouble because it contained top-secret material, the commander had no choice but to notify security. It would only be worse if she didn't and the top-secret material came to light of day.

———

The Naval Criminal Investigative Service sent its top gun, Ches Kaiser, from DC to grill her. They met in a drab room at LAAFB and sat across from each other at a gray, metal table. A squat, ugly guy in a rumpled gray suit, Kaiser got right to the point. "Commander Heartworthy, you are guilty of a high level security violation: losing custody of top-secret information."

Surprised by his bluntness, Commander Heartworthy said, "I am very sorry about this incident." And she tried an explanation, "This information was locked in my car's trunk."

"No excuse," replied Kaiser, without changing his scowl, "especially as you had given your car over to valet parking so you could party with your colleagues."

"What's wrong with valet parking?"

"It seems," said Kaiser snidely, "that the valet parking service had the keys to your trunk."

"I admit that…"

"Were you drinking?"

"Yes, sir," she said, now feeling the interview was going badly.

"What and how many."

"Three Jumboritas."

"Now tell me, what is a Jumborita, Commander Heartworthy?" he asked derisively.

She said in a subdued manner, "It is a double margarita."

Kaiser leaned back in his chair and asked, "Do you have any excuse for your actions?"

"I believe it is important for a leader to appear where the war fighters gather…"

"Why is that?" said Kaiser, leaning forward and putting his elbows on the table.

"To build team cohesion and give thanks for a job well done," she replied.

Kaiser looked at her quizzically at first, and then said firmly, "That concludes my interview. Any questions?"

She asked, "What could happen as a result of this infraction?"

"Best case: a letter of reprimand," said Kaiser.

"And worst case?"

"Demotion and forfeiture of benefits or even discharge from the service," Kaiser replied, looking at his watch.

"What can I do to mitigate the punishment?"

"Usual antidote for fucking up is to deliver superior performance," he said. "There's always reluctance to beat up on a hero."

She stood up, tried a contrite smile, and asked, "When will I hear the NCIS decision?"

"You will be notified in one to two weeks."

"Thanks, Mr. Kaiser," she said and left—feeling rotten.

Next day Commander Heartworthy personally delivered documented evidence of El Jefe's loan to Amparo, to the

Department of Justice office in downtown LA. Additionally, she provided documentation, listing several times that Amparo visited El Jefe's hacienda near San Miguel de Allende and describing her role in handling his funeral arrangements. She requested that all US accounts of Amparo Terrasombra and Mitchell Alexander be frozen, and requests for freezing assets in Mexico be processed.

——

Two days after the NCIS interview the commander noticed a *National Enquirer* headline in a supermarket checkout line that read: "CIA Eavesdrops on Fidel's Confession." The teaser on the cover said: "The near-dead narco criminal Fidel Terrasombra gave his confession to a priest not knowing that a bird-size CIA drone was recording everything. Read full Top Secret confession, inside page 20."

She knew right then things could only get worse. Her attempt to nail Amparo and Mitch with drug connections wouldn't surface in time to deflect the barrage of bad press right around the corner. She took leave for a week to await developments.

And things did get worse, as shown in a sampling of headlines over the next five days:

Der Spiegel's front-page headline read: "If You Thought NSA Eavesdropping on Angie Was Outrageous—Check Out What the CIA Is Up to Now!" The German magazine article reasoned that CIA bird bot technology could spy on people in their homes with worse threats to privacy than the NSA listening in on Chancellor Angela Merkel's cell phone.

Mexican TIME printed this headline: "Yankees Violate Sovereign and Personal Dignity." The magazine's cover picture of a bird hovering near a priest kneeling next to a man lying on the ground told it all.

El Universal's headline read: "Fidel Terrasombra Freed from Jail," The newspaper described how the judge dismissed all charges against the accused narco personality after the sensational revelation of high-tech spying on Fidel at death's door while talking to his confessor. "Basic principles of human justice prevent prosecution with evidence surreptitiously taken while a man is baring his soul to God," said Judge Jorge Uribe del Toro. A front-page picture showed Fidel leaving prison in a wheel chair. There was a bottle of tequila in his left hand, and his right hand was raised in a "V-for-victory" sign.

The headline of *L'Osservatore Romano* read: "Vatican Recalls Apostolic Nuncio from United States." The lead article of the Vatican newspaper announced it would recall its Apostolic Nuncio for consultation. The article explained that this action was prompted by the recording by a CIA robotic bird of a Catholic priest hearing the confession of a man on the edge of death.

The headline of the *New York Times* read: "Commander Heartworthy Walks the Plank!" The *Times* quoted the president at his press conference announcing the officer's firing, "A security breach at this level cannot be tolerated."

Chapter 48

ELMWOOD APARTMENTS

Gunnar Huegelmeyer was looking out the window from the thirty-sixth floor office of his Century City law firm. From his perch high above Avenue of the Stars, he was taking ten minutes for his daily morning meditation. It was six thirty and quiet. No one else was in the Huegelmeyer and Associates offices to disturb his energy flow. He watched the morning sun poking through the marine layer clouds and illuminating patches of the Hollywood hills.

Seeing the phone light flashing, he answered, "Good morning, Gunnar Huegelmeyer here." He was glad he got at least six minutes of meditation in.

"Gunnar, this is Mitch Alexander. Amparo Terrasombra suggested I call you."

"Yeah, Mitch, I read in the *LA Times* that you flew in yesterday."

"That's me, same guy, but I wish you had not read it in the friggin' newspaper."

Gunnar swiveled around to avoid the panoramic view and to focus his mind fully on the phone call.

"Amparo told me about you. What's up?"

"I need a place to live."

"Where you living now, Mitch?"

"I've got a place in the Brewery Lofts downtown."

"What's the problem there?" Gunnar wrote a few notes on a yellow legal pad with a ballpoint pen.

"Got reporters bugging me, my place here is a dump, and I have fears of Mexican narco criminals after me," said Mitch, sounding edgy.

"You need a place where no one knows where you are."

"Roger that. Got any recommendations?"

"Yes I do," said Gunnar. "Elmwood Apartments."

Mitch, his voice sounding less anxious, asked, "Where are they?"

"They're on the Westside—Culver City, in a gated complex with ten-foot-high fences and surveillance cameras. Security patrolled twenty-four seven. Inside there is a food market, pool, sauna, and usual executive apartment stuff. Touring celebrities live there, as well as newly divorced guys and people with other reasons to stay out of sight."

"Any vacancies?"

"Mitch, I have an apartment there for general-purpose use of my clients—it is available for you and Amparo for the next three months. Long enough to get you through her big exhibition and then some."

"You're a lifesaver man," said Mitch with a sigh of relief. "When can I get the key?"

"Meet me at the Petruccio restaurant in Culver City—noon. Lunch first, then we go to the Elmwood; I'll show you around and give you the key. You can move in today."

———

At Petruccio, a hip spot in the Culver City art scene, they had a quiet table in the garden out back. Mitch said, "You look a lot different than I imagined."

Gunnar chuckled. "Iron helmet and horns, maybe?"

"Yeah, your name took me in that direction, but you are shorter than six foot five and darker than I would have guessed. Not the type for raping and pillaging."

Gunnar responded, "At five foot ten, I am nothing to be concerned about. I am a LA guy born and bred. Peruvian-Japanese mom and German dad. Went to Long Beach State for engineering and Loyola for law. Speaking of names, I would never have guessed that a guy named Ricardo Casa DeSpiritu would be taller than me and blond like you." Then he raised his wine glass and proposed a toast. "To diversity and its many surprises."

Mitch had to chuckle at that, drank some wine, and got serious again. "That name thing is worrying me."

Gunnar said, "Amparo told me about the circumstances surrounding your nom de art. You have got to be prepared for what might happen when your real identity is revealed."

"I am scared shitless," admitted Mitch.

In a comforting tone, Gunnar said, "You don't have to be, because artists have worked under different names or anonymously for centuries. Not that you are trying to deceive anyone, nor have you done anything illegal. It was a really strange series of events that was the reason for your using a pseudonym. Now the game has changed and you are going to tell them who Ricardo is."

"Got all kinds of bad thoughts," Mitch said, "about what people will think when Ricardo Casa DeSpiritu is revealed to be another LA guy, born and bred."

"Mitch, there are already a lot of weird rumors about your disappearance. Like maybe it was staged for publicity, government cover-up, terrorist implications."

Mitch, looking rattled, said, "Crazy…"

Gunnar said, "You must to learn to ignore it. If there is some legal aspect to what others print or say about you and you need legal help, I am here to provide it. Otherwise just ignore it."

Mitch leaned forward. "I am just concerned about people thinking I am a con man or cheat, that there was a disappearing act to milk a lot of money out of the Ricardo Casa DeSpiritu mystery."

"There will be people who accuse you of that."

"Didn't ask to be kidnapped…"

"You know how it all happened. In your heart."

"Gunnar, if I could just sit down and explain it…"

"Too soon. Keep away from the press. Tell your story when you want and how you want."

"It's weirdly complicated."

"That's why you need time to figure it all out and make sure every potential question is anticipated and you have answers. Right now your story is furnishing the nut-fringe with rant-and-rage opportunities. You need time for the lunatics to forget you and go on to their next windmill to attack."

Gunner showed Mitch the apartment after lunch and told the Elmwood manager about Mitch staying there and his need for absolute privacy. Mitch agreed to meet Gunnar the next day at his office to go over details of the exhibition involving intellectual property.

Mitch moved into the apartment that afternoon and called Doc Philorubius. "Remember me?"

"Oh Gawd, as I live and suck air!" Burt roared. "Mitch, it's you!"

"Yeah, Burt, Dream Wreckster has returned."

"How are you feeling? Still freakin' out at night?"

"Not anymore," said Mitch, loving the down-to-earth sound of Burt talking. "Not since I've been liberated."

"Hot dog! Man, I want to get together with you. Want to hear about where you've been and see how you look."

———

They arranged for lunch in Century City the next day, right after his 11:00 a.m. meeting with Gunnar. Doc showed up with Chad and Surfer. Doc gave him a bear hug, and the other two gave him perfunctory man-hugs. Mitch said, "Guys, I've just met with my lawyer, Gunnar Huegelmeyer. He said I am going to be besieged by people wanting to interview me, to write articles, to write books, to be friends, and to support causes. I'm not doing any of that stuff. I am going to tell you guys some of what happened, but I ask you not to pass it on. Anyone you run into that wants info about me—tell them to call Gunnar."

"So, what the hell ya been doing south of the border all these months?" asked Surfer. "We didn't know if you were dead or alive. I'll bet Burt did, because he met us one day and told us he had a feeling you were OK."

"Yeah, guys," said Burt. "I had a feeling he was OK."

"You had more than a feeling." Surfer snorted. "You were holding out on us Burt, you tricky, little, psycho jockey."

Burt, with arms crossed, leaned back with a cherubic smile, unfolded one arm, and gave Surfer the finger.

Mitch said, "Guys here's the five-thousand-foot story," and went on to overview what happened while he was gone. His story was interrupted by exclamations of: "*Submarine—*no shit; a *chain*—no fuckin' way; Sierra Gorda—never heard of it; shoot out—damn; beautiful girlfriend—wow; I'd take my chances with a kidnapping for that."

Raucous laughter erupted.

Chad said, "Mitch, you got to paint with us at the beach."

"I want to, guys, but not going to the old places," said Mitch.

"Why not, Dude?" asked Surfer.

"That asshole Fidel still thinks I ratted them out and got his brother killed."

Burt asked, "Isn't he banged up physically?"

Mitch said, "That prick is out to get me. I've dealt with him up close. He is friggin' crazed. Not sure he is out of the game—banged up or not—so I'm playing it safe."

Chad popped in, "Let's paint at the Santa Monica pier. He'd never think of you being there."

"Good idea," said Burt. "Mitch needs some time to unpack mentally after living on the run. He can go back to Malibu when the time is right."

Chad said, "Sunday, nine a.m. Park on the pier and walk out to the end. We'll meet you there."

————

Mitch's e-mail draft for Amparo that night said: "Amparo dearest, Returning to LA was a blast of joy and sadness. Joy to see old friends. Sadness to be away from you. Can't wait to see you. Use our secret e-mail system until I feel less paranoid. This e-mail is coming from a public library not far from our new living quarters.

"Gunnar fixed us up with a secure apartment in Culver City. That's on the West Side of LA—you'll love it. Let me know when you are coming up here for exhibition arrangements.

"I am still nervous about vague and dark threats. What's real, what's imagined? Who knows? Is Fidel a threat? A drunk three thousand miles away? Doesn't seem likely. Are my old war demons still hanging around? Did living under the radar in Mexico push me in a weird direction? Whatever it is, Burt said to just stay in my comfort zone and time will take care of the rest. Problem is that I'm not a comfort-zone kind of guy.

"Enough about me. Got a bunch of questions for you about how the LA exhibition is shaping up. Most important, how are you weathering the storm? Any bad vibes from the Terrasombras? Anything I can do to help from up here? Need any more paintings from my studio?

"I don't like publicity, crowds, stuff like that. But I'm no longer the guy right off the submarine. I grew some mental elephant skin in Mexico and think it's tough enough now to handle the exhibition and all that goes with it. I am still anxious and a little depressed about pulling the covers on Ricardo Casa DeSpiritu. If I were standing next to you I'd say I am just rambling and don't pay any attention to me.

"Let me hear from you pronto in a long e-mail—so I can read it over and over. *Te amo mucho*, Ricardo."

Next day Mitch found this e-mail from Amparo: "Mi Amor, I am busy the total day. I read your message several times, because your words remind me of the beloved rebel that is on my mind all the time. You can help by taking ten early Dream Wrecks from your studio to Constalli framers on Pico Blvd. They are expecting them. Don't tell them who you are. Best you have a low profile until the big night. Better for your brain and better for our business.

"As you Americans say, I am working my buttocks off. So much to do. Gunnar and his lawyers are a big help with business details. Happy he got a safe place for you. I am looking forward to love nesting when I come to LA in a week.

"*La Familia* is going about their business. Some of them want to know who tipped off the government that Tio Max was at the hacienda. Family loyalty is a big deal here, even if someone in the family is bad, turning him in is not a healthy idea. I see a few cousins sometimes for lunch but am working night and day. Avoiding family and friends as much as possible. La Señora is very sad, and that hurts me, because her heart is so good. She is living in our old family home in Morelia with my mother and brothers. The government has confiscated the hacienda near San Miguel that she loved so much. Fidel is with the family in Morelia also, healing from his fall. I have not seen him and don't want to either.

"Government investigators interviewed me. Don't know what they are looking for. Maybe a drug connection. They told me that someone inside the hacienda killed Tio Max! I couldn't believe it. Autopsy results. What does that mean? I can't begin to think who. Or maybe I must start thinking in the direction that we were in a criminal world there. No more denial. Those close to Tio Max were there because they did what bandits do. One of them killed him.

"They said the second picture you painted is evidence! Hate the thought of La Señora and me there next to the evil brothers, in some government office. Fortunately La Señora's portrait was released and I sent it to her."

"Mi Amor, I think you should start looking for a place to live around LA. We might need a quiet place after Pensamientos Febriles III. *Con mucho amor*, Amparo."

Chapter 49

DANGEROUS AGAIN

Barely a week after the shootout in the Garden of James, Fidel was released from jail. He turned down all requests for newspaper and TV interviews, preferring to live in the shadows where he was comfortable. No way he wanted public attention. He knew there were no guarantees of safety in life—and even fewer with your face splashed all over the papers.

His thirst for revenge against the artist, like his thirst for alcohol, was stronger than ever. He burned with feelings of hatred against Mitch, just as he knew others did against him—others among the many that had been run over by the Terrasombras when they were in power. He knew too that there would be a new generation striving for power that wants to make sure the old-generation men were out of the way. Didn't need publicity to remind any of these guys that he was living the good life with a get-out-of-jail-free card. Besides he wanted a quiet place to heal and get out of the wheel chair. The family home where he grew up in Morelia was that place.

Checking the Internet news from his laptop, the convalescing Fidel found that Mitch was back in LA. Now to find where he was living—and where he was painting. He phoned the Brewery Lofts that he had seen on the Internet news and was told Mitch was living at an undisclosed location. No help there. Then there was Amparo, that traitorous bitch; she would know where he is.

In her gallery she was selling his crazy abstracts. Ugly stuff, but anything passes for art these days. She was with Mitch in the garden where he got shot. *After everything that Maxi did for her, she is banging the guy got Maxi killed,* thought Fidel. *I'll take care of the artist first, and then there will be time to take care of her. She'll regret hooking up with that hijo de puta. But now I'll keep away from her so she doesn't know how much I hate her. But I'll be listening in.*

Using his underworld connections in Mexico City, Fidel had Amparo's gallery phone tapped and recordings of her calls sent to an Internet drop box. Every night he accessed the recorded calls from the family home in Morelia. He hated listening in on a lot of chickenshit art gallery calls, but he quickly found that hearing fifteen or twenty seconds of most them was enough to know if they were worth listening to further. This way he could check a day of Amparo's calls in just twenty minutes. That was bearable.

After a week of eavesdropping he heard the call he was waiting for! Fidel heard Amparo answer the phone, "Buenas tardes, Galeria Amparo."

The speaker on the other end of the line said, "Mi Amor, I can't wait until you come up to LA in a couple of days."

"Careful what you say on the phone, Mitch."

Fidel thumped the table in triumph.

"I couldn't wait to e-mail you."

"What is so urgent?" asked Amparo.

"I'm painting people now."

"Mitch that's a big change for you."

"The fishermen at the Santa Monica pier are a great subject to paint. Great to see a bunch of human beings working at such a basic thing as fishing."

Another table thump. Fidel knew where he could find that hijo de puta.

"How do you get the people you're painting to stop moving?" asked Amparo.

Mitch laughed. "They spend a lot of time just standing still, looking at the water."

She said, "Be careful, Mi Amor. Fidel is free now. Probably not ready to travel, but still we don't want him to know where you are."

"This is a good place to paint for a month until the exhibition. It is away from my old haunts at Malibu. No one recognizes me here."

Thanks, hijo de puta, thought Fidel. *There will be one person who will recognize you.*

Chapter 50

LOVE NESTING

Mitch picked Amparo up at the Tom Bradley Terminal. The old blue Honda made a better impression than he thought it would. When they wheeled the baggage cart up to its trunk, Amparo said, "This is a suitable car for a man that lives for his art and not the materialistic distractions in life."

Mitch chortled and replied, "I love it when you talk dirty."

Slipping into the passenger seat, Amparo asked, "How far to the Elmwoods?"

Twenty minutes got them there.

Amparo said, "Mi Amor, I plan to stay four nights to take care of business meetings."

Mitch replied, "I'll try to make it interesting for you when you are not racing around to meetings and lunches." And handed her a glass of wine.

"Thank you," she replied and looked around. "I like this place; it's romantic."

Amparo took the barrette out of her hair and shook it loose so her face was softened and framed in glistening black waves. She sipped the wine and Mitch unbuttoned her blouse and unsnapped her bra. She said, "I've been waiting all day for that, Mi Amor, and you didn't let me down." Arms around each other and intense, deep kissing when the doorbell rang: the Chinese food delivery.

Then a kaleidoscope of sensations: abalone in celestial cinnamon sauce; jasmine tea; Peking duck; gewürztraminer wine; starry night above the bubbling, steaming Jacuzzi; locked-in bodies; fireworks of love; music wafting through; deepest kind of sleep; and…morning sunshine sneaking in with a new day.

———

Mitch showed Amparo the Santa Monica pier in its funky splendor. They walked past the merry-go-round, seafood restaurants, amusement rides, and arcade with it ringing bells and raucous noises. Mitch pointed out scenes along the way where he had been painting. Showed her the fishermen, lost to the world around them, intent on pulling the occasional creature out of the sea.

The Jamaican sketch artist captured them side by side in charcoal for twenty bucks. He asked when Mitch was coming back to paint again.

"In a few days, after I show my lady around," Mitch told him. "Might even do a painting of you."

"That will be cool, mahn. Then we have a beer."

Down the stairs from the pier parking lot, they rented an umbrella and beach chairs and peeled down to their bathing suits. The ocean was cold at first but invigorating once they were in and swimming around. Mitch tried to teach Amparo to ride waves. She struggled and took on a lot of saltwater before they decided it would take a few more sessions. After a jog down the beach, they flopped in their beach chairs and soaked in the sights of passing beach people and the sounds of pounding surf.

Mitch told her he phoned his father two days before. First time he had spoken with him in over ten years. Back then his dad was an abusive drunk, but he cleaned up his act five years ago and married a woman he met at AA. Mitch said his father was still sober and sounded surprisingly good. He was glad for him and glad he called to try letting go of the residue of bitterness he had been lugging around for so long. By the end of the call, they had promised to keep in touch.

"You did something right when you called your father," said Amparo. "I could love you just for that, Mi Amor. None of us are perfect, and we have to forgive."

After enough serious talk, they bought corndogs and lemonade. A walk down the promenade to Venice Beach in a stream of bikers, skaters, skate boarders, scooter kids, strollers, wheel chairs, joggers, and walkers—while watching Muscle Beach weight lifters; street performers of all kinds, including the famous chain saw juggler; and assorted crazies—put them in humanity overload.

A restorative snooze preceded dinner with Gunnar and his wife, Murielle, at the Ivey on Robertson. Celebs are were frequently seen there, and their evening was no exception: Bill Clinton was at a nearby table. The waiter told them on the QT that the Ivey was his usual dining place while in town. Amparo, straining to hear, reported that he ordered vegan. When his party was about to leave, she zipped over to Clinton's table and got his autograph, beating out the herd of autograph seekers that was heading his way from most of the other tables in the room.

Snuggling in bed that night, Amparo told Mitch he had the same attentive look and smile that Bill Clinton had.

He replied, "Autograph in the morning."

The next three days were busy for Amparo with appointments and conference calls. They managed to fit in lunch with Burt Philorubious at the VA hospital cafeteria. They went to the Brewery to check his inventory of Dream Wreck paintings and dropped in to say hello to Kathy. She and Amparo hit it off. Amparo found people like Burt and Kathy straightforward and candid—a break from her art world with its eternally unanswered aesthetic questions, self-promotion, and studied outrageousness.

————

The last night together was quiet. Amparo was wiped out from full days of work on the Pensamientos Febriles III exhibition. She was satisfied things were on the right track and could relax. Mitch wanted to spend some time discussing their life after the big show. They walked back from dinner at Petruccio's and were sitting on the apartment balcony. Mitch lit a candle to make up for the escaping twilight glow.

They kissed and then sat there looking into each other's eyes. Amparo looked away for a moment and said, "There is something I must tell you now." She looked back at him and said, "I tried to hint at it in my e-mails to you, hoping to get it out in the open."

Mitch sensed a cloud in the happiness of the moment. "Tell me, Amparo. What is it?"

She put her hand on his. "I was the one who tipped off the army, causing the raid on the hacienda."

A baffled look appeared on Mitch's face. An uncomfortable pause. He asked, "Why didn't you tell me sooner?"

"Let me try to explain," she started. "I was desperate to find a way to prevent Tio Max from killing you. That's all I could think of—calling in the army to arrest him."

Mitch said, "After the raid in San Miguel, we told each other everything…"

She said, "At that time I couldn't even face the fact that my betrayal of Tio Max got him killed. I just wanted that dark secret to disappear."

"But, Amparo, you saved my life."

"I had to, Mitch; I couldn't live and let you die."

"Didn't you trust me enough to let me know you put it all on the line for me?"

Tears ran down her face. She held his hand and said, "Let me tell you more. I hope you will understand."

Mitch, looking serious, said, "OK, you've got the floor."

Amparo continued: "I was afraid that if the word got out that I denounced Tio Max, it could cost me everything—my family's affection, possibly my business depending on the press coverage, and maybe even my life. That fear was a cloud on my soul."

"Amparo, you didn't honestly think I would tell anyone your secret?"

"Oh no, Mitch. It was just that telling you would bring that cloud that I carry—into your life. I didn't want to do that. Especially in San Miguel. We were so happy there."

"But, Amparo, that is what life serves us up sometimes. Grim stuff that we have to face together."

"How true, Mitch," Amparo said and took a moment to gather her thoughts. "Mi Amor, the fight with Fidel at the Garden of James really convinced me he was out to kill you—because he thought you were responsible for the army raid. Right then I saw my secret could endanger you—because he wouldn't be after you, if he knew it was I that called the army.

"But I didn't think it was an immediate danger because Fidel was badly hurt and had been arrested. I thought he would be in jail for a long time and couldn't get to you from there." She takes a deep breath. "Then he got out when that estúpido coast guard woman revealed his confession."

Mitch said sympathetically, "I'm getting it…your dilemma."

Amparo continued, "The exhibition will be over in a month. It will make us a lot of money, giving us the freedom to get out of the limelight and live quietly. Fidel is crippled and a bad alcoholic. Not an immediate threat to you here in America, with him deep in Mexico."

Mitch added, "You're right; he shouldn't be a problem now. Your secret is now shared by two: you and me. That's enough. We can't let it out, Amparo, because then Fidel would go after you instead of me. I'll never let that happen."

Next morning at LAX, they said adios, and she was gone.

Chapter 51

THE SECOND CHOICE

A week later Amparo flew back to LA for another ten days of meetings and coordination with the staff of the Los Angeles County Museum of Art. Her team flew in the next day. Bill Gastineau, her curator, would handle gallery space preparation, picture hanging, signage, music, and sales. Nardi Quinterez would handle shipping logistics before and after the event, insurance, and catering arrangements. Yuri Ventura would handle press releases, security, VIP coddling, endorsement contracts, and everything that fell between the cracks.

Seasoned from working on Amparo's high-powered events, they went right to work in the LACMA spaces. Amparo was a hands-on manager who met with her team every morning in person or by teleconference.

Most days Mitch and Amparo were off in separate directions. He drove to the pier to capture his new love— painting the fishermen at work. She drove to the city to keep Pensamientos Febriles III moving forward.

One day Mitch and Amparo found time to meet Chad and Surfer for lunch at the Lobster restaurant by the Santa Monica Pier. Amparo was fascinated by Chad's enthusiastic description of art therapy techniques. He explained how Plein Air Expression fits into the toolbox of art therapy methods to overcome emotional problems. She had many questions. Chad, a cerebral type, lapped up the attention of Amparo and answered them best he could.

Surfer teased Mitch about not going to Malibu Seafood any more. Mitch told them he still wasn't comfortable with that idea. Flashbacks to the submarine and the nightly leg iron were still occasional, unwelcome visitors. Mitch told the guys he would join them someday in Malibu, but right now wanted to keep away from there so as not to tempt the return of Dream Wreck nightmares. He said he would work where he felt safe—in the crowds at the Santa Monica pier.

Amparo couldn't get over how Chad and Surfer could paint and work together. She thought Chad was enthusiastic about his therapy work and was a bit on the academic side in his conversation. Surfer was the exact opposite, boisterously expressing pretty negative views about well, everything. She asked them, "Muchachos, you both are pretty different but seem to get along OK with your work and painting adventures. How do you stay friends?"

Chad replied, "It is a yin-and-yang thing. Our differences provide a dialectical synergy that we find mutually satisfying."

Amparo then turned to Surfer. "What do you think keeps you guys as amigos?"

Surfer, scratching his head with a perplexed expression on his face, said, "Beats the shit outta me."

———

The ten days of Amparo's visit raced by, with both she and Mitch fully engaged every day with work or painting and most evenings together. On her last afternoon, Amparo visited the pier to watch him capturing the fishermen on canvas. He said to her, "Painting crowds of people is a different trip than painting straight from nature. Groups of people are united by some kind of unseen interaction and it is my job to capture some of that stuff to make the painting work."

Amparo said, "I like how each person you paint is an individual with just a few strokes showing their movement and hinting at what they are like."

"That's the fun of it. Having each person in the scene contribute to the outcome of the painting," said Mitch, all the time observing the pier folks and brushing on a color note or two for each one.

That night they walked to Petruccio's for an unhurried dinner and walked home through the evening haze and fog that was creeping in from the ocean. They sat on the balcony with sweaters on and the candle flickering in the breeze.

Mitch said, "You can choose to think of fog as something gray that hides the stars, or you can choose to think of it as something that softly blocks out the world around you, making you focus on the person close to you. Your choice, Señorita."

"The second choice, of course."

"For picking the right choice, you get a prize," said Mitch as he slid a diamond engagement ring on her finger. "Will you marry me *soon*?"

"Oh! Mi Amor, you already know my answer."

They stood up and held each other silently for the longest time, Amparo said, "This ring with its sparkly diamond symbolizes a new era for us."

Mitch replied, "Well put, Mi Amor, a peaceful era of happiness and hope."

Chapter 52

SANTA MONICA PIER

Mitch was at the Santa Monica Pier, painting in front of the harbormaster's office. He had become a pier regular with his almost daily visits there. From his painting spot, he was facing the shore looking toward the lower deck at the fishermen. He was working on a large, three-foot-square canvas—the same painting Amparo had seen him working on a week ago. It was nearing completion.

A banner that read "WELCOME BACK MITCH" was hanging from the pier lampposts. On his cell phone with Amparo, he said, "I can't believe it. There are at least a hundred artists here to welcome me back. How'd they know I'd be here?"

"I am so happy for you; enjoy the day, Mi Amor."

They hung up.

"Hey, Chad," Mitch asked, "did you guys have anything to do with all these artists here?"

"Sure did, man. We spread the word at our therapy sessions that the most famous graduate would be here today."

Artist easels were set up all over the pier and were especially thick near Mitch's painting spot, as there was great curiosity about him.

Mitch didn't like crowds. But this time it felt right, surrounded by a gaggle of brother and sister artists, while he painted fishermen on the lower level. He captured with rapid-fire strokes the rituals of teasing fish with baited hooks and the thrill of reeling them in. In a good mood, he didn't mind all the people around and the many interruptions with questions.

Suddenly, he felt a jolt of panic! *I cannot frigging believe it.* There was Fidel, a hundred feet away in a wheel chair. With him, a tattooed gangbanger. "Shit!" said Mitch. "How did that asshole know I'm here?" Mitch saw Fidel pointing right at him—that started the gangbanger running out the pier toward him, crashing through the sea of artists. Other artists saw the danger and yelled to warn Mitch. The banger had a ten-inch stiletto switchblade in his hand. He was smashing his way through the last twenty feet of artists and easels when Surfer saw him.

Surfer was set up on the upper-level walkway of the harbormaster's office. Thinking fast, he picked up his entire easel, held it out above the lower deck, and then dropped it on the banger's head as he charged by below.

Mitch leapt forward as the tattooed thug hit hard on splintery old planks, dropping his stiletto. Mitch stomped the shaved head to keep him down, then picked up the knife. Mitch took off, running toward Fidel—with rage overpowering reason he was determined to kill him with the knife in his hand. Fidel spun his wheel chair 180 degrees and raced back toward the arcade building. Once inside he maneuvered through the maze of chiming machines and blinking video games, scraping screaming people and pets aside, while heading for the back door and the pier parking lot. He wheeled through the door to his waiting van.

Fidel fired a few shots, slowing Mitch, buying enough seconds for him to get out of the wheel chair and hobble into the van's passenger door. Mitch ran toward the van but the gangbanger at the wheel gunned the motor, crashed through the pay-booth barrier, screeched tires up the ramp to Ocean Avenue, and escaped.

A wheelchair with a tequila bottle in its drink holder remained behind.

The cops interviewed Mitch as well as other witnesses at the scene. Mitch told them who Fidel was and gave them the gangbanger's knife.

Mitch sat down with Surfer and Chad at an outside table by the Ferris wheel.

"Damn, that was close," said Chad.

Surfer added, "We'll get all the artists on the lookout next week in Chinatown. Anyone sees that mommy-jammer Fidel and his low riders will call the cops and alert us. Mitch, in Chinatown you'll need an escape route; no sense shooting it out in a crowd. Could hit innocent people. We'll give all the artists and cops there pictures of Fidel to keep them on their toes. No way that drunken asshole is going to drive his wheel-chair anywhere near you."

"Sounds like a plan," said Mitch and took a bite of Polish sausage. "Damn, these things are good." He called Amparo on his cell phone. "Hello, Mi Amor, we are having a great day at the pier." Clicking to speakerphone, he said, "Say hello to the guys."

"Hola, muchachos. Paint well and beautifully."

"Amparo, you missed a great day and a lot of wild and crazy people here," said Chad.

"I know artists. You're having a great time. Miss you all."

Mitch told Amparo, "Next weekend will be a blast. We're painting in Chinatown. There's going to be a big celebration there."

Mitch walked away for privacy and spoke with Amparo, omitting the news of Fidel's appearance. He thought, *I'm not going to tell her about this incident until after the exhibition. She'll be pissed off. Especially because I hassled her for not tell-ing me about her calling the army on El Jefe. But, if I tell her about Fidel being here today, she'll feel that she must reveal her betrayal of El Jefe—to take the heat off me. I can't let her put herself in that danger.*

Chapter 53

CHINATOWN

Mitch, Chad, and Surfer arrived at the Gate of Filial Piety before the crowds came to celebrate the birthday of New Chinatown.

Mitch said, "Guys, this is great; look at the colors in the buildings."

"Tough decision. What to paint," said Chad.

"Dudes, painting the plaza gets all them wild colors."

"Yeah, Surfer, but that is facing away from the parade," Mitch said. "And this parade only happens once a year. That dragon is an incredible sight."

"Yo, Dude, how ya goin' to paint it leaping' and jumpin'?"

"Real fast," said Mitch. "Paint everything around its place on the canvas first. When the dragon gets here, paint it at warp speed."

Other artists began to arrive. Chad and Surfer gave pictures of Fidel to them and put them on alert. "Call Mitch if you see him drive up in his wheelchair, then call the police on duty here or call nine one one."

Mitch was apprehensive about Fidel joining the party—but knew he usually shows up drunk and was not going to worry too much with everyone on the lookout for him.

He started on his canvas, capturing the approaching parade in broad strokes, keeping a bare space for the dragon to be painted in when it got close. As the parade was approaching, he could just see the dragon in the distance getting bigger. In spite of the noise of firecrackers and smoke, Mitch was in the zone now and had forgotten about Fidel.

———

But Fidel hadn't forgotten about him.

Disguised in a long, black overcoat, black fedora, and thick Fu Manchu mustache, Fidel slipped into Gin Ling Way from Hill Street—unnoticed by the artists and police. He limped through the alley of colorful shops toward the Central Plaza at Broadway, using a carved ivory cane for support. He was looking for Mitch. He stopped for a minute and leaned against the statue of Sun Yat Sen to take a shot of tequila. Mitch saw him first, just thirty feet away! His heart pounded in a tightened chest with the recognition of his hated antagonist.

Then Fidel saw him, and Mitch ran for it—just like he told the guys he would. He yelled to the guys that Fidel was there but wasn't heard above the deafening noise of firecrackers and pounding drums.

Fidel drew his pistol and went after him—surprisingly fast for a cripple. Mitch ran out onto Broadway just in front of the approaching dragon and ran back along its opposite side, dropping into the line of dragon runners carrying the fire-belching monster. He braced his arms along the side rails, with which the runners held the dragon aloft, and raised his feet when he saw the bottom of Fidel's coat and ivory cane moving by.

Arms killing him, he dropped his feet down to run with the other dragon runners, who were yelling, "Hey, fuckhead, get out of the dragon!"

He ducked out, looked back, and didn't see Fidel in the smoke of snapping firecrackers and advancing musicians. Dodging into the crowd on the far side of Broadway, he too melted into the sea of people.

Phoning Chad, he said, "Fidel is here. I ran away. Grab my easel and take it when you leave."

Chad said, "OK, pal, got you covered."

Mitch said, "I'll call you again to make contact and pick up my gear. Gotta run now."

He made his way back to the parking structure at the Empress Pavilion and sneaked to his blue Honda to make sure no one was waiting for him near it or in it. From there he phoned Gunnar Huegelmeyer. "Fidel showed up today."

"No!" yelled Gunnar in disbelief. "Where?"

"Chinatown," said Mitch. "We were painting during the parade."

"Thought you guys had artists and cops on lookout for him?"

"We did, Gunnar. We were expecting a Mexican guy in a wheelchair."

"What did you get?"

"Fu Manchu, in an ankle-length black coat, wearing a black fedora, and limping along with an ivory cane."

"Mitch, get serious! This is getting to be low comedy."

"I am serious, Gunnar," said Mitch, perplexed. "How did that creep know where we would be?"

"Sounds like he's got a phone tap going for him."

"Crap, I've been phoning Amparo lately, too," said Mitch, sounding disgusted with himself.

"Mitch, you're getting careless."

"You're right. Damn!" said Mitch, shaking his head. "Goin' back to our e-mail system."

"Stay away from your Brewery studio, too, even in the daytime. If you must go there, let me know, and I'll provide secure transportation and bodyguards."

"Gunnar, we need ironclad security for the Pensamientos Febriles III opening next weekend."

"You'll get it. There will be an armed defense, with police briefed about Fidel and ready but not visible to the guests. Mitch, you should stay away. That jerk tried to kill you twice in a week."

"Can't. I gotta be there," insisted Mitch.

"OK, Mitch, I'll get you covered with heavy security, but you're wearing a bulletproof vest. And I am getting a couple of bodyguards to shadow you—and a couple for Amparo too."

"Can you get me a gun permit?"

"I'll get right on it—but I doubt we can get one in a week. I am not enthused about you shooting in a crowded hall. So don't count on carrying a gun."

"You're right, Gunnar, but the bodyguards and security must be briefed and ready to take down Fidel if he shows up." Mitch then added, "Uh, Gunnar, don't tell Amparo about Fidel being in town."

"What do you want me to tell her?"

Mitch said, "Tell her you have arranged for a ton of security to handle threats ranging from gate crashers to armed criminals. We've got to keep her mind at ease. This is her big night."

"I've got to do what is best for my client," Gunnar said firmly.

"Look, Gunnar," said Mitch, with heightened determination, "Amparo is coming tomorrow and will stay through the exhibition and beyond. If she knows Fidel is in LA, she will do something that she thinks will take the heat off me. But you must believe me; it will only increase the danger for her. I am not free to tell you what is involved, because I am sworn to secrecy."

"Mitch, you are not making it easy for me, but you too are a client," said Gunnar. "I'll respect your wishes."

"Thanks, man."

"I will work with the police and private security to provide maximum protection—as much as I would provide for my own family."

"OK Gunnar, I am counting on you."

Chapter 54

PENSAMIENTOS FEBRILES III

An über-glitzed clientele arrived in a stream of limos at the Pensamientos Febriles III opening at the Los Angeles County Museum of Art. Men in high-style tuxes milled about, enjoying the sight of incredible women in designer gowns. Security men in formal wear were prepped for alertness and briefed on the appearance and MO of Fidel Terrasombra.

Minutes after the exhibition opened, collectors snapped up early Pensamientos Febriles for a hundred thousand dollars each. Phone-in buyers half a world away sealed deals on later colorful Pensamientos Febriles going for three times that much—and the new Sierra Gorda works sold in the half-million range.

Amparo, resplendent in Balenciaga, was right at home; she talked excitedly to the press about the evolution of Ricardo's works. "It is a hopeful journey he is on—his current works have morphed from calls for help to assertions of a place in this world. And the Sierra Gorda works reflect a landscape that can be sublime or tortured—he handles both well. His humanness and freedom of soul radiate from his works, making them accessible to anyone."

Mitch, however, was uneasy. He did not want to lock into conversations that would take away his vigilance. He lurked in the background, shadowed by two bodyguards, patrolling the crowd fringes. He was wearing a bulletproof vest and scanning continuously for Fidel.

Amparo paused from conversation with reporters to read a note handed to her. A big smile radiated, and she exclaimed breathlessly before the press microphones, "I've just been handed a note by our curator, Bill Gastineau, that the exhibition is sold out! I want our friends and collectors to know I thank them from deep in my heart." The orchestra burst into the epic passage from *Jupiter, the Bringer of Jollity.*

A candle-lit dinner followed. After guests were seated, Amparo, following a drum roll, introduced her companion for the evening: Mitch Alexander, who was kidnapped and recently rescued in Mexico.

Everyone strained to get a good look at this artist who reappeared on the LA scene amid a storm of wild speculation about his disappearance. The buzz becomes thunderous as guests stood up and jockeyed for a closer look.

When the crowd simmered down, Amparo asked for quiet as she had another announcement to make. "Dear friends, at this time I want to answer the question on everyone's mind: 'Who is Ricardo Casa DeSpiritu?'" Total silence for a few moments before Amparo continued. "It is none other than Mitch

Alexander, who is with me here tonight—and to whom I am engaged to be married."

Cheers, whistles and wild yells of support were mixed with shouts and angry exclamations. The orchestra struck up the *Rocky* theme music. Gunnar Huegelmeyer took a microphone and pleaded with guests to sit down and enjoy their dinners.

An irate guest, with clip-on bow tie hanging off one collar point, remained standing yelling, "It's a rip-off! Goddamn publicity stunt!"

The cascade of shouts continued.

"Sit down, jerk!"

"God bless you, Mitch."

"You rock, Amparo!"

"Fraud!"

Applause mixed with catcalls and whistles continued. Amparo was jolted by the insults and stood speechless. Mitch stood up and put his arm around her. And the two of them faced the unruly gathering.

Gunnar, used to the raw conflicts of tough LA courtrooms, just grinned from the podium and said, "Relax, my friends; please take a seat." His strong, calming presence quelled the clamor.

———

But not everyone relaxed and took a seat. Unnoticed by security, who had not been guarding the food service elevator, Fidel approached the head table out of the churning mob of excited guests. With his hair dyed gray and wearing a fake matching beard, he was disguised as a French aesthete. Sporting a black cape, maroon beret, monocle, and a heavy, eight-inch gold crucifix hanging on a thick chain necklace, he was shuffling along with the aid of a walker. At the head table his bleary, bloodshot eyes locked on Mitch.

Gunnar on the microphone was saying, "There have been amazing life and death developments in the last year of this artist's life. As these developments become known…"

Bang, bang! Shots from two guns.

Fidel and one of Mitch's bodyguards had drawn guns and fired with instant recognition of each other. Hit in the chest, Fidel reeled backward, falling across a table of diners just starting their oysters and champagne. Mitch too went over backward in his chair—wind knocked out of him—from a hammer blow to his bulletproof vest. Security and police swept in to take out a raving Fidel, whose gold crucifix saved him from a bullet to the heart.

Bedlam ensued. Screams and shouts welled up in the hall. People ran. Fell down. Crawled to safety under tables. Then hearing no more shots, started crawling out and cautiously standing up.

The outsize buzz of an LA party resumed, ignoring the few guests headed for the doors.

Security men knelt over Mitch and confirmed the bullet was stopped, even though his breath was knocked out and ribs badly bruised.

Gunnar Huegelmeyer, on the microphone again, got the crowd to calm down.

"Dear friends, let me say that Amparo has not been harmed. Mitch is OK—wearing a bulletproof vest saved him from the assassin's bullet. His attacker was Fidel Terrasombra, brother of deceased drug lord El Jefe. Fidel is alive and in custody of the LAPD. Amparo and Mitch are in good shape. They have left the premises. Right now they need peace and quiet—but they want you to enjoy this wonderful evening and party on."

Adventure-loving guests stayed and partied on. They knew that Pensamientos Febriles III would be talked about for a long time—and they wanted bragging rights.

Chapter 55

SEIZURE

"Feds Seize Ricardo Casa DeSpiritu Holdings" screamed a *Los Angeles Times* headline. The newspaper was in a vending machine at the US Department of Justice building in downtown LA. On the steps of the building not far from the machine, Gunnar Huegelmeyer was holding a news conference. A reporter asked, "When did you first know of this seizure of the Ricardo Casa DeSpiritu Empire?"

"We learned of it this morning when I, as attorney representing Amparo Terrasombra and Mitchell Alexander, was served with a writ of seizure at my office. It ordered the seizure of all financial and physical assets of the Ricardo Casa DeSpiritu enterprise in the United States."

"Why is our government taking this action?"

"Hard to say what their motivation is," said Gunnar, looking out over a brace of microphones. "It's clearly illegal under US law—and under Mexican law."

"Please explain, Gunnar."

"OK, let's look at Amparo's half of the partnership. The government claims drug money from El Jefe's fortune went into founding her art business. It is true that El Jefe lent her money to get started when she was twenty-one years old. He was her uncle, and she was unaware of his criminal affiliation. She repaid it all in two years, and there were no further financial relationships.

"It is a fact that she did not knowingly accept drug money or launder drug money in any way, and we'll prove it. The government has no right to deprive someone of their livelihood for having received a loan in good faith from funds that may or may not have been earned illegally in another country." Gunnar paused and took a drink from a plastic water bottle. "Now let's look at Mitch's half of the partnership. He was a prisoner when they met in Mexico. Amparo did not know that. She was led to believe he was an artist guest of El Jefe, brought in to one of his haciendas to paint her grandmother. Amparo liked his work and agreed to represent him going fifty-fifty on all profits. Business flourished, and they made money. This money had no connection with narco interests. The government had even less reason to seize Mitch's assets."

A reporter asked, "Where are they now?"

Gunnar answered, "In seclusion. Not available for press contacts or interviews."

"When will Mitch Alexander tell us what he was doing in Mexico after he was liberated from El Jefe's hacienda?"

"He will be telling his story in his own way."

"When?"

"You got an insight into his story from Homeland Security. They described in detailed how they tracked El Jefe's submarine and how they rescued Mitch. You got another insight from many articles on Amparo's exhibition's of his work."

"Yeah, but when will we get Mitch's story in his own words?"

"I can assure you it is an amazing story. Mitch will tell it when he is ready to open his heart to the world."

"A lot of us feel that Mitch Alexander should tell us what happened, because millions of taxpayer's dollars were used to rescue him."

Gunnar said, "He is aware of that. He wants to do it right. That will take some time."

"Why didn't Mitch use his real name as an artist?"

"A very good quest—"

"What's he hiding from?"

"Artists can use any name they want. Ever heard of Mark Twain or Martin Sheen?"

"Can you get the Ricardo Casa DeSpiritu financial empire back?"

"I am confident we can, but it will take time."

"How long?"

"When you're up against DHS, DOJ, NSA, FBI, CIA, and DOD, it can take years."

The reporters paused, and Gunnar said, "Thank you, ladies and gentlemen." He departed without answering any of the shouted questions.

Chapter 56

TOUR BUS

Six months later:

A black tour bus, with red-and-yellow trim, pulled into the parking lot at El Pescador State Beach. Amerika Reisen was emblazoned in large letter on its sides. Tour guide, Herr Schorse, was excited—and very animated as he began to address his group of German tourists, "Meine Damen und Herren, now for the highlight of our California tour: the fascinating story of Mitch Alexander." Clambering out of the bus, the tour group was treated to the sun burning through the sea mist of a Malibu morning.

Herr Schorse, standing by the bronze statue of an artist painting at a French easel, told how Mitch Alexander, who was undergoing art therapy, disappeared from that very spot. "His kidnapping by U-boat started an astonishing adventure in Mexico, where he was imprisoned by the notorious El Jefe, escaped, and fell in love. He eventually came back to

Los Angeles with help from the US Department of Homeland Security.

"Visitors come here at all hours of the day and night. Some are artists; others are believers that nature's sights and sounds enliven human emotional and spiritual consciousness."

Herr Schorse pointed west. "Take a look over this cliff. The scene Mitch Alexander was painting when he disappeared is what you see down there. He called it Hideaway Cove—this isolated beach with a white house tucked in at the far end. Looking in the other direction, you will see a yoga group in session and a few artists painting *en plein air*. That's pretty typical; you can see yogis and artists here just about any time of day."

The tour group boarded, and the bus proceeded ten miles south on Pacific Coast Highway with Herr Schorse pointing out cliff-top estates of Hollywood stars and commenting on aspects of life in Malibu. They parked at Corral Beach.

Herr Schorse exclaimed, "We are in luck; there is an art therapy class going on right now! Since Mitch Alexander's kidnapping, this class has grown much larger—as you can see there must be fifty easels on the beach to our right. Even Hollywood celebrities are signing up for it.

"Oh Mein Gott! I can't believe my eyes. Dr. Phil is working at the easel right in front of Chad Willoughby, the chief counselor. Dr. Phil is the biggest TV therapist in America. Rumors in the scandal sheets hinted that he has psychological problems of his own. Must be true, because there he is!

"I find it fascinating that Californians will stand out here in public getting mental health therapy—not caring who sees them. Could an average Duesseldorfer do that along the Rhein with a curious public walking by? Absolut nicht!

"Now, dear friends, we will be lunching at Malibu Seafood right across Pacific Coast Highway." Their tour bus proceeded uphill half a mile, made a U-turn, and came back down to the restaurant parking lot. The group disembarked and went to a picnic table area reserved for them.

Herr Schorse told them of Mitch's tumultuous experiences after his disappearance. "Our kidnapped artist met an art promoter in Mexico, named Amparo Terrasombra. She marketed his artwork under the nom de art, Ricardo Casa DeSpiritu. As many of you know, that name was respected in the style and product marketing worlds.

"Details of Mitch's life in Mexico are still largely a mystery. Six months ago, Amparo staged an exhibition of his work at the Los Angeles County Museum of Art. The exhibition was completely sold out at the reception, which was followed with a high society dinner.

"At this incredible event, Amparo announced that Mitch Alexander was the mysterious Ricardo Casa DeSpiritu. That blockbuster news caused an uproar. But as if that wasn't enough for one night, an uncle of Amparo's tried unsuccessfully to assassinate Mitch Alexander. Uncle Fidel will be in jail for a long time."

Herr Schorse continued excitedly, "Disaster struck three days later: the US government confiscated all assets of the Ricardo Casa DeSpiritu financial empire, leaving them penniless.

"And do you know what? Two weeks after losing everything, Mitch married Amparo at Malibu courthouse, just 4.7 kilometers down the highway from here. How many of us would get married if all the money disappeared? Think it over my friends.

"They had their wedding dinner right here at Malibu Seafood. Their artist friends brought white tablecloths, candles, and wine to make it a special occasion—just as Amerika Reisen is going to do for you right now!"

Herr Schorse's two helpers quickly set the rugged picnic tables with white cloths, crystal candleholders, ice buckets, and champagne. Herr Schorse announced, "And now, meine Damen und Herren, please line up at the take-out window for the same wedding dinner our newlyweds had on their wedding night—lobster, baked potato, cole slaw, and bread pudding with beer or coffee."

The tourists carried their trays to the picnic tables and started off with a champagne toast to Mitch and Amparo—Herr Schorse raised his glass. "May Mitch and Amparo live happily ever after, wherever they may be!

"While you are eating, I am going to describe some aspects of this story that make it a never-ending subject of conversation.

"First the U-boat. It was manufactured in Norway to custom specifications of Maximilliano Terrasombra, who started an underwater excursion business with it at Puerto Rana Verde in Mexico. This U-boat had no torpedoes, allowing the space saved to be used for first class accommodations. It could take eight passengers on trips of up to two weeks. Special undersea windows and brilliant lights for the dark depths made for spectacular viewing.

"Actually, at Puerto Rana Verde the most tourists ever got was a two-day trip. It is now known this U-boat was used mainly for trafficking people and drugs back and forth to California. The special exterior making the U-boat look as if it came from a Jules Verne story was just for appearances—this was a very up-to-date vessel technologically.

"OK, enough technical information. Now for the juicy stuff.

"You all know that the abstract paintings that Amparo called Pensamientos Febriles, or Fevered Thoughts, sold for up to three hundred thousand euros. These paintings were what Mitch Alexander used to call Dream Wrecks and they sold for two hundred dollars when he lived in LA. Is that the power of promotion or are they worth that much?"

He heard murmurs in his audience.

"One of those mysteries of art, my friends."

A tour group member asked, "How long did it take to paint a Dream Wreck or Pensa...whatever you call them?"

"We've heard that it took him about two hours."

Mental calculations, and the tour group murmured some more.

"What are Mitch and Amparo doing now?"

"They are living in seclusion. Not known where."

"Does he still have legal problems?"

"Yes, the American government has confiscated their US bank accounts and all works that Mitch had in his LA studio. Their lawyer, Gunnar Huegelmeyer, is fighting to recover their assets."

"Why don't they just live in Mexico?"

"That's a delicate situation also. The Mexican government wants to know how he disappeared when they raided El Jefe's hacienda and how he managed to live in Mexico for months illegally. Also the government there isn't happy about US secret agencies operating there without telling them."

"Amparo's gallery—is it still open in Mexico City?"

"No, it's closed—as you can understand, their lives got complicated."

A tourist said, "If Mitch and Amparo just told the world what went on down there, it would explain a lot of things."

"*Jawohl*, my friends, that would explain a lot of things. Someday maybe they will."

Chapter 57

BEST SELLER

Two years later:

From the south, pelicans flew by Corral Beach in echelon formation powered by updrafts along the Malibu cliffs. Ancestors of these graceful flyers had been cruising these shores for millennia. They had seen changes in the shape of the earth below—without themselves changing. They had borne witness to the cycles of activity of the human tribe along the shore.

———

On this day the pelicans looked down on the artists at the Corral Creek Bridge and noticed the group was growing bigger with the passing of the seasons.

"I love to watch pelicans in formation," said Jane Heartworthy on her first day in Chad's group—and the pelicans heard her fifty feet overhead.

"Yar, it means good luck when they fly over you," said Surfer, as he showed her how to hold a brush.

"Let's hope it is true. I can use some good luck in my life." Those were the last of Jane's words the pelicans heard as they flew farther up the coast. Many of the pelicans in the formation had been cruising Malibu updrafts for over twenty years. They had seen more and more artists along the cliffs in the last couple of years. Lately they saw cars and catering trucks parked in every available spot along the Pacific Coast Highway.

When the pelican formation approached El Pescador State Beach, the usual crowd of visitors clicking photos surrounded the artist statue. The pelicans heard a tour bus guide announce to her group who had just disembarked, "My friends, we have a special surprise for you today. Mitch Alexander is here signing his incredible, best-selling book." A chorus of cheers erupted. The pelicans saw the guide direct her group to the line of people leading to the picnic table near the cliff's edge.

The pelicans saw Mitch Alexander seated at the table with boxes of books. They also saw enthusiastic faces of fans in a long line. They were waiting to buy an autographed copy of *Dream Wrecks, an Artist's Struggle for Fulfillment.*

Amparo Alexander, reclining in a chaise lounge nearby, put the book she was reading aside to watch the pelicans approaching. The little boy in a playpen next to her saw the pelicans as they flew overhead. He let out a squeal, causing Mitch and Amparo's eyes to meet for a moment and their smiles to bloom. The formation flyers took all this in as they glided over the red umbrella that shaded Amparo and her baby. From their altitude, the sharp-eyed flyers could see the red umbrella in a painting on Mitch's easel—the painting he worked on whenever there was a break in the book line.

After the pelicans cruised by, they noticed the white house at the end of Hideaway Cove hadn't changed at all in many seasons—except for the old, powder-blue Honda Civic and the tricycle now in the driveway.

ABOUT THE AUTHOR

Dick Heimbold is a Southern California fine artist and author. This book springs from his enjoyment of painting in the outdoors, particularly by the ocean with his buddies in Malibu. Other ingredients of this story were derived from his travels in Mexico, including painting and exhibiting his work there; his years in the high-tech aerospace industry; and his infatuation with Southern California—that he's maintained since hitchhiking in from New Jersey years ago.